"YOU are Sir Jeremy Stafford?" asked Alfreda.

"That is correct."

"Your father's name was Jeremy, too?" She seemed to be confused about something.

"No—I'm the first Jeremy in the family." He was already enjoying the interview, although he didn't know what it was leading to.

"You must forgive me," the girl said. "It's just that I was expecting a much older man than you seem to be."

"I hope you're not disappointed."

"Oh, no—just a bit puzzled."

"No more than I am, Miss—?"

Alfie's heart was thumping wildly. The moment had come. She thought for the last time of giving her idea up, but she swallowed the great lump that was forming in her throat and screwed up her courage. "Sir Jeremy," she said, barely loud enough to be heard. "I have reason to believe that you are my—," she was finding it difficult to come right out with it. "Or rather, that I am your —daughter."

ABOUT THE AUTHOR

Denice Greenlea was born in Paterson, New Jersey, and was raised in a small town in Bergen County near New York City. She attended Northwestern University, majoring in theater and creative writing, and there met her husband, a British student working for his doctorate in geography. She now lives in Albany, New York, with her husband, who teaches at the State University, and her two cats, Sylvie and Bruno. She is active in local dinner and community theater and finds acting a satisfying complement to writing. This is her first novel.

The Fortune Seeker

Denice Greenlea

A FAWCETT CREST BOOK

Fawcett Publications, Inc., Greenwich, Connecticut

THE FORTUNE SEEKER

A Fawcett Crest Original

© 1977 Denice Greenlea

ISBN: 0-449-23301-4

Printed in the United States of America

10   9   8   7   6   5   4   3   2   1

The
Fortune
Seeker

1

"THESE damn balls," Sir Jeremy Stafford remarked conversationally. The statement required no reply save that of a sympathetic grunt, which Arthur Huxtable duly granted. The two gentlemen stood inconspicuously in an alcove that afforded an excellent, if somewhat peripheral, view of the ballroom. The dancers were lining up for an old-fashioned quadrille, waiting only for the music to start before beginning their intricate steps. An occasional high-pitched giggle rose above the genteel hum of conversation and clinking glasses.

Sir Jeremy breathed a sigh of relief as the music finally started. "How I escaped this dance I don't know," he said. "My sister must be running out of eligible misses to introduce me to. Besides being boring, these balls seem to be unnecessarily strenuous when one is obliged to keep up with partners half one's age."

Arthur Huxtable chuckled. "If you showed up at more than one ball a season, perhaps Cecily could spread the young fillies out more evenly, instead of presenting 'em to you all in one lot, as it were."

"If I had the choice, I wouldn't show up at any balls, and then I could avoid these young fillies, as you so nicely put it, altogether."

"Come now, Jeremy, it can't be that bad," Arthur said, then he added a bit wistfully, "I wish I had the opportunities you have. That little one in the pale blue seemed rather nice, for instance."

"Too young and too insipid for my taste, and I believe my nephew, John, has first claim to her. He was looking very fierce when I led her to the floor."

"Ah, well, you're the catch of the Season, you know."

Sir Jeremy raised an eyebrow. "My dear Hux, I have been the catch of the Season for seventeen years, and I assure you it is due more to my inimitable pocketbook than to my inimitable charm." Here, despite his words, Sir Jeremy gave a rather charming smile. "Besides, I prefer to do the catching if there's any to be done, which is why I avoid the hooks so carefully. Don't forget, I've been caught once before and I can't say I cared for it overly much."

"You're just too choosy," Arthur said, looking out at the ballroom again where the dance was coming to an end. Although he tried to sympathize with Sir Jeremy's attitude, he himself was having a rather good time—that is, whenever he found someone short enough to dance with. Unfortunately, this seemed to be a Season for tall beauties, and while Arthur enjoyed dancing, he knew he looked ridiculous with a partner several inches too tall for him. He glanced at his friend, easily one of the tallest men in the room, and reflected for a moment on the unfair distribution of Fortune's favors. Why, there stood Sir Jeremy, tall, handsome, rich, titled—any woman in the room would fall eagerly into his arms if he so much as raised an eyebrow at her, and he didn't want any of 'em, except perhaps one or two who were already safely married. While here stood Arthur himself—willing, eager, possessing a reasonable competence and a pleasant London house, but too short and with a stoutness that even the best tailor could not disguise. Arthur sighed as he glanced at the trim, athletic form of Sir Jeremy who, even with his carelessly tied cravat, presented a figure of easy elegance. Arthur felt no envy toward his friend, but it did seem a great waste.

Suddenly he gave Sir Jeremy a sharp poke. "Look out, here comes your sister with some fresh bait."

"I certainly hope it's not another schoolroom chit whose only subject of conversation is the new baby princess. I already know more than I care to about the Queen's whelping habits," said Sir Jeremy with a long-suffering air.

Cecily, Lady Chandler, was making her way toward them, shepherding a small, freckled, shy-looking girl in an unremarkable white dress. Sir Jeremy cast a sly wink at Arthur, who knew that meant no good for the girl and immediately felt sorry for her.

"Why, Cecily," Sir Jeremy said expansively when his sister finally reached them after exchanging bits of conversation with everyone in her path, "you're a perfect vision tonight in that seafoam green, I must say." Lady Chandler's eyes narrowed with slight suspicion at this somewhat effusive compliment. "And who," Sir Jeremy continued, "is this charming creature? Cecily, I beg you to introduce us. I've been waiting for an introduction all evening."

This last was addressed to the young lady herself, who blushed uncomfortably and fixed her gaze on the hem of her dress.

Lady Chandler would gladly have boxed her brother's ears, but since she was not precisely in a position to do so, she merely said, with icy charm, "Jeremy, I would like you to meet Miss Mary Ellen Jennings. I believe you knew her father."

Sir Jeremy smiled graciously and, bowing to the young lady, said, "Miss Jennings, your father and I were in school together. But I thought he had gone to India to seek his fortune in the regiment."

Lady Chandler did not appreciate being reminded that she was once again introducing her brother to someone nearly young enough to be his daughter, but she had an obligation to the girl now. "Well, Jeremy, Colonel Jennings has found his fortune and returned to England. In fact, I believe he has purchased a house quite close to Stafford Hall. Isn't that right, Miss Jennings?"

The girl nodded, but still did not dare to raise her eyes to Sir Jeremy.

"Yes!" he exclaimed suddenly after a thoughtful silence. "I remember your father well, though he was a few years ahead of me. 'Inky Arnold' we used to call him—because he was always very inky, you see."

Arthur Huxtable cleared his throat. "May I have the honor?"

Lady Chandler gave him a grateful glance. "Mr. Huxtable, Miss Jennings."

Miss Jennings looked up at Arthur and curtsied very

prettily, in spite of her freckles.

"Would you be so kind as to grace me with your next dance, Miss Jennings?" Sir Jeremy inquired, holding out his arm.

Miss Jennings gave one last frightened glance at the hem of her dress and took Sir Jeremy's arm. Lady Chandler and Arthur Huxtable watched them as they walked out to the floor.

"Really, Hux, it's just too bad of him," Lady Chandler said, stamping her foot in frustration. "Inky Arnold, indeed!"

Arthur Huxtable thought it best not to reply directly to this remark. "Lovely ball, Cecily. But your balls are always lovely."

It didn't work.

"Don't change the subject, Hux. Can't you *do* anything with him?"

"Do? I?" Arthur Huxtable was at a loss.

"Talk some sense into him."

"My dear Cecily, I would if I could, but—"

"I know, I know. He's never listened to anyone in his life—but at least you could *try*."

"For you, Cecily, I'll try, but I'll make no promise."

"Goodness knows I try," she said, a slight pout wrinkling her still attractive mouth. "I've been trying for years. I've introduced him to every eligible female between the ages of fourteen and forty, but nothing seems to work. He gives them one dance apiece—if that—and then goes off and spends his time with someone like Lady Foxwood, who's survived two ancient husbands and would certainly never marry Jeremy should Foxwood drop dead, since Jeremy's much too young for her taste. He just keeps her amused while she tries to spend three fortunes. It seems Jeremy will only pay attention to those women there's no chance of marrying. You'd think he'd feel obliged to make sure he had an heir. I'd hate to see Stafford Hall go to a total stranger, but he doesn't seem to care."

Arthur gave a low chuckle and Lady Chandler turned on him angrily. "And just what is so funny about that? Do you *want* to see Stafford Hall pass to my fourth cousin twice removed, or whatever relation that dreadful man in Worcestershire happens to be?"

"No, Cess, it's not that at all." He chuckled again. "It's just that Jeremy's about two feet taller than your latest attempt and they do make a pair."

Lady Chandler watched the dancers for a moment, her brow still creased with agitation. Indeed, Sir Jeremy almost had to lean down for the poor girl to reach her hand to his shoulder as they waltzed. Fortunately, despite his dislike for the occupation, Sir Jeremy had always been a graceful dancer, so the result of his bent position, although peculiar, was not disastrous. Lady Chandler had to smile, though. "You're right, Hux, perhaps I should be more discriminating in the future. If it weren't a waltz, they wouldn't look so odd—I must be sure to introduce the short girls to him only for the country dances."

Arthur's smile faded as she spoke. "Dunno, Cess. P'rhaps you're right. Not about the country dances— about the other thing. Sometimes I think you're trying too hard and putting him off even more, but now and then I think a nice little wife would be just the thing for Jerry."

"I wish Jeremy could see it, too. Why, he's the only one who doesn't think so."

"I will put a word in his ear for you, Cess. As I said,

I can't make any promises, but I'll do my part. Try and make him see it's for his own good, that he should forget about breeding horses for a bit and breed an heir, that sort of thing."

Lady Chandler smiled gratefully. "Do, Hux, do. Why, if I could get him settled down, my mind would be easy— and perhaps I could concentrate my energies on you."

Arthur brightened at this. "That's an idea, Cess. Forget about the country dances altogether for Jer and leave the short girls to me. For instance, I think I'll ask this Miss Jennings to dance. I'm more her size—and I'm not old enough to be her father, as Jeremy is."

"You're a dear," Lady Chandler said, and Arthur was rather inclined to agree, though it wasn't just to please Cecily that he wished to dance with Mary Ellen Jennings.

Unfortunately, later Arthur found it difficult to keep his word to Lady Chandler. As he and Sir Jeremy were waiting for the carriage to come around, Arthur was hard put to get *any* word in—let alone the one Lady Chandler desired him to—because Sir Jeremy was rambling on and on about the boredom he had suffered, the various inadequacies of his dancing partners, and the general disagreeableness of leaving Stafford Hall in the first place just to please his sister.

This often seemed to be the way between the two of them. Sometimes Sir Jeremy would speak to Arthur merely so people wouldn't think it odd if they found him talking to himself. Arthur didn't mind, really, but it was a nuisance when he had something of his own to say. To do Sir Jeremy justice, though, he was quite willing to lend an ear to Arthur—when finished with his own piece. In fact, he often sought Arthur's advice or opinion on some small matter, and even if he didn't find the advice itself worthwhile, Arthur often unintentionally said something useful.

That was very nearly how they had met about nine years before. Sir Jeremy had been up to London to look at some horses in which he was interested and he was staying at his club, as was his habit. As he sat in a comfortable chair, thinking about the good and bad points of the various horses he was looking to buy, he turned suddenly to Arthur, sitting nearby, and said, "What do *you* think—does that chestnut have speed or just good looks?"

Arthur knew who Sir Jeremy was, of course, although they had never been properly introduced, Arthur being a very recent member of the club. Not wishing to appear stupid before such a renowned sportsman and judge of horseflesh, he had replied, "I wouldn't want to say anything definite about the chestnut, but the bay is another matter."

The fact that there was no bay in the lot did not mar Sir Jeremy's enjoyment of this reply. When he had finished laughing he began a conversation with Arthur, which had resulted in an invitation to Stafford Hall and a long friendship. Though not usually one to question the reason of things, Arthur did sometimes wonder what it was that made their friendship last. There was a common interest in horses and the two frequently attended the races together or engaged in other gentlemanly pursuits, such as partridge shooting and fox hunting, but beyond that there seemed to be few mutual interests. Arthur had none of Sir Jeremy's interest in literature and, not owning any land of his own because of the wasteful habits of his forebears, he had no interest in the day-to-day problems of running an estate that constantly beset Sir Jeremy. But Arthur was quite willing to listen to these problems and eventually he grew to look on Stafford Hall as his second home, thus enjoying the delights of an estate directly and the headaches only indirectly. He had long since concluded that he and Jeremy simply enjoyed each other's company, and there certainly could be no better basis for friendship than that.

Right now, though, Arthur had a different problem—what could he say to Sir Jeremy that would convince his conscience that he had kept his word to Lady Chandler? He noticed that Sir Jeremy was finally winding up his tirade, having finished his quota of complaints for the evening, so he took a deep breath and said, "Jer, don't you think it was coming it a bit strong with that Inky Arnold stuff?"

Sir Jeremy laughed. "I thought Cecily deserved it."

"Yes, but the girl, Jer, the girl."

"Sorry—you're right, of course. It was hard on the girl." He looked extremely penitent for a moment until Arthur caught a mischievous gleam in his eye. "We did call him Inky Arnold, you know—it was as if he washed with the stuff."

Arthur gave up and joined him in a hearty laugh as the coach drew up. Well, he could tell Cecily he had at least reprimanded Sir Jeremy as far as he was capable of doing so. And if his conscience were not satisfied, he could always bring up the subject of marriage some other time, perhaps when Sir Jeremy was in a more serious mood and thus more open to suggestion. They stepped into the coach, and as Arthur settled back comfortably against the cushions, he lost himself in more pleasant and personal thoughts.

"Where to, Hux—home or club?"

"Eh? What?" said Arthur, startled out of his short

reverie. "Oh, home tonight, I believe—I'm a bit done in."

Sir Jeremy gave the appropriate direction to the coachman and then turned to his friend with an inquisitive glance, noticing a certain faraway look in Arthur's eyes. "Don't tell me some fair damsel has smitten you already, and this only your first ball of the Season."

"And most likely your last," Arthur returned.

"Well, perhaps not if I must keep watch on you. The noble race of bachelors wouldn't wish to lose one of its finest supporters."

This remark was not calculated to improve Arthur's humor, as Sir Jeremy well knew it was mostly his size and not choice that kept Arthur a bachelor.

"Well, if I found I didn't care for being married, I could always send her packing just as you did," Arthur retorted, and immediately regretted the remark as he saw the look of pain that crossed Sir Jeremy's face. "Sorry, Jer, that was unkind."

"Yes, and not precisely accurate either, since she needed no sending. But I can't expect you to know that—it's ancient history and you were a mere lad of thirteen at the time."

Arthur tried to make further amends. "Lord knows your reputation has been impeccable ever since. That is, besides a few actresses or dancers, who don't count anyway since they're not proper ladies, and perhaps one or two married—"

"That's enough, Hux," Sir Jeremy said with a laugh. "I have no desire to call up all my ghosts from the past." The two then fell into a comfortable silence, which was only broken when Sir Jeremy inquired whether Arthur would be returning to Stafford Hall with him the next day.

Arthur looked surprised. "No—that is to say, I didn't realize you'd be going back so soon."

"Well, I intended to stop at Tattersalls, just so my trip up wouldn't be wasted, but of course I'll be returning in the afternoon. I have three horses entered in the county races this summer, and while I trust Jamie to the utmost with their care and training, I feel obliged to keep my eye on them. You must come down and see the new black I've purchased from Windon. He'll be giving them a run for the money or I'm no judge of horseflesh."

This did sound like a tempting prospect to Arthur since he knew Sir Jeremy certainly was a judge of horseflesh, but he shook his head and said, "Sorry, Jer, but I promised my mother I'd stay on for at least two weeks." He smiled. "It will be my turn to be introduced to all the young ladies, or so Cess promised—providing, of course, they're not more than about four and a half feet high."

"Well, Hux, speaking from my own experience of this evening, I wouldn't say there were any exciting geese in the gaggle."

Arthur gazed out of the window at the passing houses. "Oh, I wouldn't say that, Jer, I wouldn't say that."

Sir Jeremy raised an eyebrow. "Why, Hux, I believe I was correct before."

Arthur affected a look of innocence. "Correct about what? I daresay you were correct about *something*—you usually are—but there's no need to be so mysterious about it, you know."

Sir Jeremy smiled crookedly. "If you don't wish to speak of it, just say so, Hux. I certainly don't mean to pry. But I wish you luck, despite what I said before."

Arthur dropped all pretense and smiled warmly. "Thanks, Jer. She's ever so nice, you know."

2

ALFREDA Marsh dragged her feet as she walked along the sunny Paris streets. Although it was a beautiful spring day, she didn't notice, for she walked with her head bowed down and saw nothing but the few feet of dull pavement that lay ahead of her. She was mentally adding up the few francs she had received from her pupils that day and subtracting the amount she could give to her father without his wondering where the rest had gone to. The little bit she kept to herself she would place safely in a drawer, tied up in an old stocking. She privately called this her escape fund, because when the stocking was full, she would escape from the large and lonely city of Paris to set up a small school of her own in a small and friendly French village, or perhaps even in England. She wasn't quite sure yet how her father

19

would fit in with this plan, but there was plenty of time to think about that, for her savings were not great and did not promise to become so for a long time. One did not become rich by teaching a few French children how to speak English.

She noticed a park bench out of the corner of her eye and sat down, glad for the rest. When she finally looked up, she saw for the first-time that the flowers had all bloomed and the birds were tending to their nests. She took a deep breath of the fragrant air and suddenly felt better.

"Alfie Marsh," she reprimanded herself, "you'll be an old lady by the time you're thirty if you continue like this." After taking another deep breath and a long stretch to relax her tense muscles, she leaned back on the bench and just savored the day, something she hadn't done for months. The sky was sparkling blue, and the birds and flowers gave bright spots of color to the green trees and grass; some children were playing in the distance. The city was in its glory and it was possible for anyone to forget personal troubles for a few minutes and revel in the sweetness nature offered.

"Look—it's spring, Alfie," she told herself. She giggled suddenly and said out loud, "It's springtime, but it's winter in my heart." She liked the sound of that and made a little song of it as she stood up and started walking homeward again.

"It's springtime outside, but winter in my heart," she repeated to herself, keeping in time with her steps. She gave a little skip whenever she came to the "winter in my heart" part, and anyone watching her would not have taken her for the same downcast girl who had sat on the bench just a few minutes before.

Indeed, Alfie was not unusually dispirited—her active mind and vivid imagination rarely allowed for that—but she knew the extreme ups and downs of living with a gambler, which her father was. Unfortunately, the past few years had been a steady series of downs and Alfie had found it necessary to take on French pupils to make ends meet. She had been teaching for more than two years now and was beginning to think of it as a permanent way of life. At least it was something she enjoyed doing—that is, when she had a bright pupil to work with. Alfie herself had always thirsted for learning, and perhaps because she had never been to a proper school or had a governess for more than a few months at a time, she delighted in reading any and all books that came her way. Her education might be considered better than that received by most young girls, particularly her counterparts in Victorian England, for her reading was never monitored —she had never been told that anything she read was unsuitable or unnecessary for a girl to know. She had read books on history, science, and mathematics—all fields that were considered superfluous to a woman's education—and had even taught herself a bit of Latin and Greek. Thus when she realized she must do something to make some money, she immediately thought of teaching, for she was certain that nothing would give her more pleasure than to share her knowledge, and perhaps learn something new herself.

Her father had been shocked when he first learned what she was doing, but his arguments that the Marshes had always been a noble family held no weight when it came time to pay the rent. He soon reconciled himself to the idea of Alfie's teaching, more readily than she would have thought possible. In fact, after a while he

took it as a good opportunity to stop trying his luck at
the gaming tables so often. He learned to enjoy sitting
at home with a bottle of cheap French wine to keep him
warm, and even found it a relief not to have to keep up
the good appearances necessary to allow him entrance
into the best clubs where the best money was to be found.
His occupation had taken its toll on his health over the
years, and now, with the promise of permanent poverty,
he grew thinner and grayer as the days went by.

At first Alfie had been happy that gambling had finally
lost its charm for him, but her fond visions of her father
settling down to a decent occupation soon vanished. The
natural laziness that had led to his chosen pursuit in the
first place, with the idea of getting rich in the easiest possible manner, now prompted him to do nothing more
than lie around all day, thinking about the world with a
wine-inspired philosophy. Alfie often wished now that
he had not given up the gambling life; at least then he had
been out in the world—charming, active, dispensing
money generously when he had it. Bad luck and too much
drink had made him indolent and parsimonious, begrudg-
ing every penny Alfie spent on clothes, food, or any
other necessity that did not directly contribute to his personal comfort.

Thus it was no wonder there was winter in Alfreda's
heart. She held cherished memories of better days that
had been filled with gay balls, beautiful gowns, and expensive hotels. At one time there had been five young
men at once who desired to marry her, and her father
could afford to refuse them all. "Damn frogs!" he would
say. "They think they're good enough for a Marsh, do
they? You just wait, Alfie, until someone worthy of you

comes along. An Englishman is what you want, with good English pounds."

But no one worthy—or no one her father thought worthy—had come along. At first Alfie herself wouldn't have minded one of the "damn frogs." She thought them silly and affected, but they were also gracious and some were rich—French francs, admittedly, but lots of them. And a few had even sported dubious titles derived from guillotined ancestors. She had her romantic dreams of falling in love, of course, but having been raised in France, she had been inclined to the French view that marriage and love don't necessarily have to come together—in fact, it is often preferable that they don't.

There had been one Englishman in her ranks of admirers, but he was someone Alfie would rather forget. Indeed, she had spent many months trying to do just that, but even now the very thought of the man made her feel somewhat ill. She had been very young at the time, barely eighteen, and her father was in the middle of a long spell of good luck. They moved in some of the best circles of French Society and Alfie enjoyed herself tremendously. She was always very popular as a dancing partner since she was vivacious, beautiful, fashionably tall, and renowned for an occasional very witty remark. Unfortunately, these were also the attractions that brought her to the attention of a certain Damon Whitfield.

Whitfield was a kind of colleague of her father's, being a gambler himself, but he also dealt in more unsavory pastimes such as blackmail and extortion. It was an ill-kept secret that he had made his fortune from the bad luck of others, and while people were polite to him for fear of becoming his next victim, it was doubtful he was liked anywhere.

Alfie's own dislike of him had been intense from the moment they were introduced.

"Alfie, Mr. Whitfield has been wishing to meet you for some time," Robert Marsh had said, trying to close up the silence that had resulted when Alfie backed away from Whitfield's rather ostentatious effort to kiss her hand.

Alfie mumbled something incoherent, something to the effect that all her dances for the evening were promised. She had not liked the look in Whitfield's eyes, but what was worse was her father's anger on their way home that night.

"You might at least have been civil," he said. "Whitfield is a very important man."

"I'm sorry, Father, I just don't like him," was all she could say, and all she continued to say whenever she met Whitfield. Unfortunately, this was more and more often as the weeks went by. Her father seemed to encourage the scoundrel, although he knew that the very sight of him was repulsive to Alfie. He practically forced her to dance with Whitfield at the many balls they attended. There was no malady Alfie could plead that would release her from this fate, although more than once the headaches and stomachaches were genuine. Alfie had had some small experience with getting rid of undesirable suitors, but none of her usual tactics seemed to work with Whitfield. The more she told him she disliked him, the more he seemed to seek her out. If she was sarcastic and biting, he admired her wit; if she was uncommunicative, he gave her fruits and inquired if she was ailing.

At last Alfie could stand it no longer. She knew both Whitfield and her father had matrimonial plans for her and she would not tolerate it. She would sooner die than

marry Whitfield, but when she told her father so he could
not believe her.

"Aren't you being a bit melodramatic, my dear?" he
had said.

"Father, I am being truthful. If I must marry Whitfield,
tell me now so I may end my life immediately. I cannot
stand to have him hanging about me any longer. He is
rude and conceited and ridiculously pompous and fat.
And," she added, as if she were producing the most
persuasive argument of all, "he has thick lips."

Her father's answer was almost a whine. "I just don't
understand you, Alfie. I won't deny he's what might be
called stout, and I never really noticed his lips, but—
hang it all, Alfie, Whitfield's a rich man, an Englishman.
He can buy you anything you want. And he loves you—
he told me so himself."

"He may have told you so, but he does *not* love me,
Father." Alfie looked at him with a straightforward gaze
that made Robert Marsh extremely uncomfortable. "You
may think me too young to know of such things, but I'm
afraid you have made me grow up a bit too quickly. What
Whitfield feels for me is not love. Certainly he desires
me—I'm sure he does—but, Father, you know the man.
I would be exciting to him as long as I resisted, but once
he had me under his control, he would tire of me. Death
is infinitely preferable to a life as one of Damon Whitfield's discarded whims."

Robert Marsh had tried to close his ears to what she
was saying, for he wished to deny the truth of it. He had
forced himself to believe that Whitfield's intentions were
honorable since he offered marriage, that Whitfield's feelings were more than mere lust. But Alfie was right, Robert
Marsh did know the man, and when he had to hear this

from his own daughter, he was disgusted with himself. Lord knew he was no saint, but he was not such a devil as that.

"I'll do my best, Alfie," he said wearily. "I'll see to it he doesn't bother you again."

If he lost all, Alfie's look of relief and gratefulness and her affectionate hug would have been reward enough. It was not easy for him to extricate himself from Whitfield, for the fact was he owed him money, a great deal of money. But while Robert Marsh would gladly have given his daughter in marriage to wipe out these debts, he was not so callous as to force her to marry someone she absolutely loathed, someone who would degrade her, as Whitfield undoubtedly would. Fortunately, at that time he still had some important and wealthy friends and managed to make up the sum from a dozen different sources. When he was finally able to tell Whitfield to go to the devil, he had a stroke of luck, for Whitfield had been meddling with the wrong people and was forced to leave Paris anyway.

Alfie's safety from the man was assured, but it took her a long time to forget Whitfield's leering glances, his clumsy attempts to touch her, the malodorous aura of tobacco that forever clung to him. One thing the experience had taught her was that she could never marry anyone just for money, that she could not sell herself for a secure financial position. All through her life she had been aware of the importance of money because of the times they were without it. In her experience, money meant security; but while she was still unclear as to what love was, she knew somehow it was not a thing money could buy, nor was it merely Society gossip of who was keeping whom, nor was it the feeling Damon Whitfield had held for her.

And so, while she could not define it in positive terms, she was certain she would know it when she found it and that it would be more exciting and wonderful than anything she knew or imagined now.

Alfie enjoyed Society life for several more years, as her father's luck managed to hold. She received dozens more offers of marriage, but although some of her suitors were pleasant and not unattractive, she knew she did not love them and often she could not help but see a shadow of that feeling that was not love but something more bestial in their eyes, which invariably reminded her of Whitfield.

But by now all her beaux were long gone and long forgotten, undoubtedly married to suitable Frenchwomen and unlikely to rescue her from her present situation. She was becoming nearly too old to think about marriage anymore, and was certainly no longer in a position to meet eligible men, and so had almost, but not quite, abandoned her youthful dreams of falling in love. At twenty-five her thoughts had, of necessity, turned to making a career of teaching and finding the financial security she knew existed, if not the uncertain security of romantic love.

She longed to return to England for this end, but her escape fund held barely enough for the passage, let alone enough to set up a school or even keep her until she could find a position as a governess or schoolmistress. Besides, she had no friends in England, whereas she was gradually making contacts through the French parents of her pupils, and when the time came, she might seek their aid. Also, it seemed that her father would not—or could not—return to England, and even though she thought about it often, she could never leave him. Her last vestiges of affection had been nearly wiped away by the constant smell of alcohol, but when she remembered that he had once been strong and supportive and had given her whatever he could when he could afford to do so, she knew she would always have a duty toward him.

Still she yearned for the England of her childhood. She had spent the first seven years of her life on the Marsh estate, with a pony to ride and a mother who dried her eyes, held her in warm arms, and listened to her childhood confidences. Her mother had been lost through sickness, the pony and estate in a gambling game, and she and her father had come to France with some strange woman Alfie had never met before and who had died shortly after their arrival. Even now she didn't quite understand who this woman was, and she supposed she never would. And, Alfie thought, her dreams of returning to the England she remembered were probably as unfulfillable as her dreams of falling in love.

Alfie neared the little boardinghouse she and her father were currently residing in, her steps still dancing in time to her little song. She hoped her father would be reasonably sober tonight, then she might read to him and talk to him; it was so lonely otherwise.

As she opened the rather dingy front door and stepped into the even more dingy and dismal hallway, she sensed that something was wrong. The concierge was standing at the top of the stairs, wringing her hands. When she saw Alfreda, she burst into loud wails.

Alfie flew up the stairs, calling out anxiously, "What is it? What has happened?"

The woman only wailed the louder.

Alfie grabbed her by the shoulders and shook her vigorously. "What *is* it? Stop this moaning and tell me!"

"He's dead," the woman cried, and she pointed to the door of Alfie's room.

Alfie, expecting the worst, ran to the door and flung it open, to see her father lying on the small sofa, to all appearances in a peaceful sleep.

3

"WELL, Hux what do you think?" Sir Jeremy slapped the gleaming side of a tall black horse.

"He's a beauty all right," said Arthur Huxtable. "D'you think he'll come up to scratch?"

"He must—I have all of Stafford Hall riding on him."

Arthur grinned. "Pull the other one, Jer. You'd sooner sell every horse in this stable than give up the Hall."

"You're right, Hux," Sir Jeremy said with an answering smile. "But I do have a not unsubstantial sum riding on him. I think he can do it—I know he can do it. Just look at those muscles. I can't say I've ever seen a finer piece of horseflesh."

"Can't say I have either," Arthur replied dutifully. "But what would you say to some lunch now? I'm done in."

"An excellent idea, I would say," said Sir Jeremy. "You will be able to tell me all about your month in London." He gave the horse another affectionate slap, reluctant to stop admiring it and go on to more mundane things, such as eating. "Jamie," he said to the groom as they were leaving the stable, "don't you overfeed that horse. I want to keep him sharp and trim for the race. I think he has all the weight he can stand right now."

"Sir!" Jamie's tone meant that he knew how to look after the horses as well as Sir Jeremy—if not better.

Sir Jeremy chuckled. "Come now, Jamie, I know you spoil him."

Jamie gave a toothy grin. "Aye, I suppose I do, Sir Jeremy, but if ever a horse deserved spoiling, it's that one."

Arthur, fearing another treatise on the strong points of the black while his lunch was waiting, gave an indiscreet cough.

"Sorry, Jamie," Sir Jeremy said, "here's one horse who won't stand not being spoiled and overfed."

Lunch was usually a hearty meal at Stafford Hall, especially when Sir Jeremy spent the morning riding over the estate, as he had today. The two men were so hungry from their morning's ride that they didn't even bother to change from their mud-splattered clothes before sitting down and doing full justice to the five courses that were presented to them.

Finally finished with his meal, Arthur Huxtable leaned back with a satisfied sigh and lit a cigar.

"Splendid as always, Jer, but I'll never understand how you can put down meals like this all the time and still look as if you haven't eaten for weeks."

Sir Jeremy, also leaning back in his chair, glanced lazily

at the rather rotund form of his friend. He smiled slightly. "It comes of clean living, Hux." He reached over to light a cigar. "Clean living and the fact that I'm a good foot taller than you."

"Bosh," Arthur said, exhaling a large ring of smoke. "I live as clean as the next man, and it's you who's above average in height, not I below." Sir Jeremy raised an eyebrow and Arthur added hastily, "Well, not much below."

"Then it must be all that champagne you consumed at those interminable parties and balls. I must say, I admire your fortitude in that respect, Hux. It's all I can do to force myself to attend Cecily's annual ball, and you've been in London for an entire month."

"Yes," Arthur said, his eyes dreamy. "Has it been only a month?"

"Aha!" Sir Jeremy leaned forward with a sudden spark of interest. "Who is she?"

"She?" Arthur repeated loftily.

"Let's have it, Hux, you're not a very good liar. Someone eminently suitable, I imagine."

"Oh yes, her reputation is unimpeachable." He grinned. "As a matter of fact, she hasn't had the time for it to be otherwise."

"Robbing the cradle, Hux?"

"Perhaps—oh, she's *out*, of course. How else could I have met her?"

"Pray, tell me about this charming damsel." Sir Jeremy settled himself back in his chair as if ready to listen to a long and interesting tale. He took a few puffs of his cigar.

"Well, there's nothing to tell, really. She's not beautiful

in the ordinary way, you know. More like a little robin. Very intelligent, too."

"Intelligent, you say? I must meet her. An intelligent woman would be quite refreshing."

"Oh, she is refreshing." Arthur became enthusiastic. "Why, she can quote Shakespeare—you know, a rose by any other name and that sort of thing—and she even speaks some French."

"How's her Latin?"

"Her Latin? Come, Jer, I said she was intelligent, not a bluestocking."

Sir Jeremy gave a crooked smile. "No offense intended, Hux, but I'd prefer a bluestocking, as you so delicately put it, to a young lady freshly filled with classroom knowledge." He took another thoughtful puff of his cigar. "Unfortunately, excepting my mother, I've never known what I would call an educated woman."

"Just as I've told you, Jer—you're too picky by far. You're looking for what doesn't exist. Why, a woman just isn't suited to that sort of thing."

"You underestimate the fair sex, Hux. I believe a woman's mind can be every bit as good as a man's—if she wants it to be. But in our society it's just not convenient to allow the women to know too much. The women realize this and behave accordingly, while the men go on thinking it's a deficiency of the sex, and enjoy their own superiority. The whole charade is rather amusing when you come to think of it, and I suppose it is convenient for all involved. And that," he finished with a flourish of his hand, "completes my lecture for today. If you enjoyed it, I will gladly give another tomorrow on any subject of your choosing."

"Oh, that's all right, Jer," said Arthur, a little con-

fused. "You're over my head anyway. All I know is that
Mary Ellen—"

"Mary Ellen?" Sir Jeremy raised an eyebrow. "Not the
charming Miss Jennings?"

Arthur gave him a belligerent look. "She's a sweet
girl, Jer. I won't hear a word against her."

"Why, Hux, you mistake me. I was quite overcome
by the charming Miss Jennings. Her intelligence was re-
markable, as you said, and her conversation was sparkling.
In fact—"

"That's enough, Sir Jeremy." Arthur Huxtable stood
up with considerable force, smashing his cigar out for
emphasis.

Sir Jeremy stood up with him, surprised into contrition
by his friend's outburst. "Forgive me, Hux," he said with
none of his usual sarcastic tone. "I didn't realize it had
come so far." He held out his hand.

After a slight hesitation, Arthur grasped the hand and
shook it.

"You must understand, Hux, that my actions are partly
prompted by envy. I do wish I could find happiness with
a nice simple girl instead of searching for my silly idea
of the perfect woman."

"Well, Jer, that's your business, of course. A nice
simple girl, as you say, may be just what you need. But
you know best, Jer, you know best."

"Do I, Hux?" Sir Jeremy sat down again, suddenly
feeling very tired. "Yes, you would think at my age I
would."

"But I know you would like her, Jer," Arthur went
on, settling himself comfortably again. "She's ever so
sensible, you know, even if she hasn't the kind of intelligence you're looking for. Puts a fellow quite at ease."

"I see I shall certainly have to become better acquainted with her, Hux. It seems she has more to offer you than the fact that she's the proper size."

Arthur chuckled, for talk of his lady fair quickly put him back into a good humor. "That recommended her to me at first, of course. Mary Ellen comes just up to my eyes, and she makes me feel as if I want to protect her, and I can't say it's a disagreeable feeling. She don't put on airs, either, for all she's spent her life in an exotic country amongst heathens and such." Once he found he had Sir Jeremy's attention, Arthur continued in this manner until their cigars were finished and their lunches settled. Sir Jeremy found it a pleasant enough way to pass the time, and he enjoyed hearing his friend speak with such enthusiasm on a subject other than the meal they had just consumed, as was his usual habit.

Later that afternoon, Sir Jeremy sat alone in his study. He had taken care of the day's accounts and was ready to enjoy the latest installment of a new novel that had come in the morning post. He had discovered, to his amusement, that Arthur had come down to Stafford Hall mainly because it was a mere ten miles from the Jennings' residence. Evidently, Mrs. Jennings had taken a nasty tumble, resulting in a broken bone, and was forced to leave London before the end of the Season to convalesce in her country home. Where Mrs. Jennings went, it seemed, the rest of the household was bound to follow, so Arthur was able to combine his usual visit to Stafford Hall with a close proximity to his loved one, whom he set out to visit as soon as he had changed into something more appropriate for courting than muddy riding clothes.

Thus Sir Jeremy was left alone with his thoughts, and these turned naturally to his friend's newfound happiness.

He was glad Arthur had found a romantic interest. He needed a wife and family, for he found none of the pleasure in more intellectual pursuits that kept Sir Jeremy from thinking of his own loneliness. Arthur valued his visits to Stafford Hall as a chance to escape from his own London house and his aging, somewhat petulant mother, but he needed more than Stafford Hall. He was cut out to be a family man, and it seemed that if things continued as they had begun, he would soon be pursuing that happy occupation.

Sir Jeremy remembered when he had believed himself cut out for a family man, although he had long since abandoned such ambitions. His marriage had been so many years ago and so short-lived that he could scarcely recall what it had been like to share his home with a woman. For too long a time, seventeen years, Sir Jeremy had lived the ideal bachelor's existence. He rarely went to town, and when impelled to go for business or one of his sister's balls, he spent most of his time in his club or in the private chambers of some fair and easy woman. His idealistic expectations of life had never been satisfied, and it was only his ability to laugh at himself that prevented him from becoming totally embittered. Instead, he looked on his life as rather amusing on the whole, perhaps a subject for one of the "Ages of Man" cartoons that occasionally adorned the illustrated papers. The pain of his ill-founded marriage was nearly gone, and except for an occasional pang at the innocence he had lost and would like to recover, were it possible, he rarely thought about that episode in his life.

He had been nineteen, fresh out of the university and determined to enjoy his first London Season. At that time, the balls had been wonderful to him, and his sister, already married with two babies in the nursery, had endeavored to introduce him to every young lady she knew, even as she did now. It was an exciting time, but most exciting was the glorious Caroline Lanphier, who was taking the town by storm for the third Season in a row.

Sir Jeremy fell in love with the vivacious Caroline, as dozens of men had before him, with all the passion and innocence of his extreme youth, and to his surprise and joy, Caroline Lanphier encouraged his advances wholeheartedly. He had hardly dared to hope that she would even pay attention to him, for she was two years older than he and her golden hair and bright blue eyes attracted the attentions of much more worthy men than Sir Jeremy thought himself to be. From Caroline's point of view, though, he was quite acceptable—he had already come into his title and most of his estate, the rest being contingent on his majority, of course, so he was a not totally undesirable *parti*. But while she suffered his attentions and accepted his numerous gifts of flowers and books, she refused his repeated offers of marriage, preferring to keep him eager and guessing, as were her other suitors.

At last Caroline discovered herself to be in some financial difficulties as she had overextended herself at cards, and thought Sir Jeremy's estate might come in handy. With no one to advise him but his brother-in-law, Lord Chandler—who had never been proof against a Stafford—Sir Jeremy was tumbled into a quick marriage with the fair Caroline. He was ecstatic and in love and truly believed he was the luckiest man in England.

Caroline, on the other hand, lost interest in her hastily acquired husband as soon as her debts were paid. She was bored by Sir Jeremy's earnest but fumbling love-

making. She was disgusted to discover that he often pre-
ferred his books and estate to a ball or party. As much
as he had enjoyed London Society life, he felt that it was
all properly over with and now he wanted to settle down
to his idea of perfect married life. Unfortunately, the
lovely Caroline was not interested in domestic affairs or
literary discussions. She wanted to continue to sparkle
in London Society, dazzling all the men at the balls,
riding through the park in a white habit on a black horse,
sporting more feathers in her hat than any other fashionable lady. She did not find attractive the prospect of
paying calls on the other country wives, where frowns or
giggles—of envy, she had no doubt—would greet her
London finery, or worse yet, of bringing cups of hot
soup to ailing farmers' wives and contributing needlework
to the annual fête. While Sir Jeremy's estate was only
about thirty miles from London, to Caroline it seemed
like the wastelands of Siberia, if indeed she had ever
heard of that place. And on top of all her other hardships,
she had not realized before she married just how much
of Sir Jeremy's fortune was tied up until he became twenty-
one. She was not certain she could survive two more
years before she had all the gowns and jewels she felt
deserving of, especially if all her time must be spent
cloistered in Stafford Hall, as she had been during the
first interminable winter of her marriage.

Sir Jeremy, wrapped up in his own thoughts and as-
pirations, was oblivious to his lovely wife's dissatisfaction.
He was not upset by the fierce arguments they had over
the many bills the fashionable Caroline acquired. There
were bound to be disagreements at first before they became used to each other, he thought—he would just have
to be patient. Why, he could remember arguments be-

tween his own parents that had only served to strengthen their marriage in the long run. He was living in his own dreamworld marriage, where everything was perfect and all would have a happy ending, once they sorted out their initial differences. The knowledge that Caroline was expecting a baby made his world complete, and he was preparing to enjoy a long and happy married life.

But suddenly the exquisite Caroline disappeared, leaving no word or clue as to what might have happened to her or where she might have gone. A number of the family jewels were discovered missing shortly after her disappearance, but instead of concluding the obvious, Sir Jeremy believed they had been stolen by the same scoundrels who had either kidnapped or murdered his beloved wife.

He employed Bow Street Runners to search for her, but a year went by before he heard any news. Then it was to learn that Caroline had died in childbirth; the baby—Sir Jeremy's daughter—had died shortly thereafter. The jewels had gone to pay more gambling debts, both her own and those of the man she had run off with.

Sir Jeremy's dream was finally shattered. It had taken him a very long time to recover from the blow, and even so there was something in him that he thought forever lost. He still held ideals of how he would like his life to be, but he knew now that the ideals would never be realized. As much as he wished it, he feared it was too late now for him to find the kind of wife he had always longed for and begin his life again.

Oh well, he thought suddenly, breaking out of his reverie, I'm glad Hux has met his match even if I haven't met mine. He smiled at the thought of Arthur's falling in love with Mary Ellen Jennings. He had obviously seen

more in the little robin than Sir Jeremy had noticed at
Cecily's ball that night, but Sir Jeremy was certain that
upon closer acquaintance he would find her as delightful
as Arthur made her out to be. Sir Jeremy sincerely wished
his friend happy.

4

ALFREDA Marsh had been trying unsuccessfully for half an hour to break the lock on her father's strong-box. The key had been lost years before, but before she discarded the box, she wanted to make sure there was nothing important or valuable inside. So far she had broken three hairpins, one hat pin, and an old pair of sewing scissors that were already the worse for wear, but not the lock.

Alfie was preparing to leave France and travel to England, finally fulfilling her long-standing desire to make her way in the land of her birth. Before her father had died her escape fund contained barely enough for the passage, but when she discovered a forgotten hoard of her father's, the amount of money she had was tripled, even after she paid the outstanding bills. She had laughed

41

when she discovered her father's money, crammed into the toe of an old boot. "Hoarding must run in our blood," she had said to herself, tucking it into the stocking that contained her own small sum. "We're just a family of ferrets."

By now nearly everything was ready for her long-awaited voyage. Her passage was booked and she wanted only to do some shopping before she left in five days' time. The prospect of spending even a little money for new clothes was delightful to her, because it had been such a long time since she'd had a new dress. For the first time in years she pored over pictures of the latest styles and watched the fashionable ladies strolling on the promenade, noting the bonnets and sleeves, which had changed considerably in the few years since Alfie had been fashionably dressed. She invented a hundred smart outfits in her mind, picking and choosing among them until she had planned a trousseau fit for a duchess at the very least. She knew the reality would be very limited in comparison to her imaginary wardrobe, but thinking of such things gave her pleasure and took her mind off her uncertain future and painful past.

Quite to her surprise, as she had thought their possessions meager in the extreme, it had taken her quite some time to sort through her father's personal effects, deciding what to keep, what to throw away, and what might be sold to advantage. Of course, the decisions took the longest time, as when she came across some well-loved books that might fetch a few francs if she could bear to part with them. But then her practical side would come to her rescue as she realized she hadn't enough room in her one case to carry much more than the barest necessities. She was almost finished now, having left the strongbox until last with the hope that she would discover the key somewhere before stronger measures to open it were required. But the key was nowhere to be found, so in a last desperate attempt, she placed the box on the floor and jumped on it with all her weight. Instead of breaking the lock, however, she found she had crushed the top of the box and broken the hinges. After that it was a simple matter to bend the lid backward and open it from the wrong side.

It contained just what she had expected—a lot of loose papers, among them some old letters from her mother to her father and various other things her father had thought important enough to lock up. She was a bit disappointed, though, since she had hoped to find some money, perhaps even a few English pounds. Then something shiny caught her eye and she reached for it eagerly. It was a heavy gold locket, tarnished and somewhat bent by her leap onto the strongbox. She opened it and discovered, as she expected, a woman's face, but it was not her mother's face, as she had also expected. She remembered her mother well, for all the years it had been since she saw her last, but this face was unfamiliar. It was an elegant miniature, delicately executed, and the subject was extremely beautiful. Alfie examined it carefully, but it stirred no memories for her. Perhaps the identity of the face could be discovered in one of the letters, so she looked through them again, this time more carefully.

Most of them, as she had first noticed, were love letters between her father and mother, dating from before their marriage. She read a few of them with interest and realized for the first time that her parents' marriage had been a love match. It was something she had never considered before, and somehow reading these letters brought her closer to her father than she had ever been while he was alive. She began to understand how he had come to gamble his estate away. After his wife died, nothing had mattered anymore. Possibly their removal to France had been for her father a removal from unhappy memories of his wife's long sickness and death. The letters themselves were beautiful, and it was no wonder Robert Marsh had thought them precious enough to lock away in a stout metal box.

But soon Alfie came to one in an unfamiliar hand, and opened it with quickened interest. It was brief and to the point.

> Tonight. I can no longer survive with a man who values his books more than he values me. I will be ready. I bear your child.
>
> > Caroline

Alfie felt suddenly that in breaking into her father's strongbox she had broken into his private life as well, discovering things she should never have known, but the mystery was too interesting to leave unsolved. Her father was dead now and would never know that Alfie had discovered things better left hidden. She read the letter through again, but nothing new could be gained from a second perusal of those three short lines. She glanced again at the signature.

Caroline. The name was familiar to Alfie. She looked at the face in the locket again and suddenly remembered the original. Caroline! The woman who had accompanied them to France so many years ago. She had been expecting a child—Alfie's half-sister or brother, it would seem. Alfie must have been about eight at the time. She recalled a great deal of excitement going on—the doctor coming in and out, a broad-faced peasant woman staying with them for a few days, the pitiful wailings of a newborn baby. But most of all she could remember her father's stricken look, for she had tried to comfort him when he kept muttering, incomprehensibly, "She told me it was mine." None of it had made any sense to Alfie at the time, but now the pieces began to fall into place. This woman had been unhappy with her husband—that much was obvious from the note and from vaguely remembered snatches of conversation that Alfie had not understood at the time but which in retrospect gained new meaning. Caroline must have told Alfie's father she was expecting his child, and he, devastated by the loss of his wife and land, had perhaps seen a possibility of happiness in this event. But somehow he had discovered the child was *not* his, perhaps it came too soon. No matter, both baby and mother had died, and the whole episode had remained muddled in Alfie's mind as part of the general strangeness there had been in leaving the home she had always known and coming to France.

Looking through the letters once more, she found yet another that gave light to the little mystery. It was from her father to someone she had never heard of.

Sir Jeremy Stafford, Bart.   November 28, 1825
Stafford Hall
Sussex

It is my misfortune to have to inform you that your wife died in childbirth just three days ago. I hope that your grief may be somewhat dispelled by the knowledge that you are the father of a baby girl.

As I'm sure you would wish your daughter to have all the advantages of growing up as a Stafford on your fine estate, I would be most glad to ensure that she is brought to you to be placed under your fatherly care. If you would send the necessary funds, I will arrange for her passage under the care of a competent nursemaid.

Once again, I offer both my condolences and my congratulations.

Robert Marsh

It was a strange letter. Alfie could picture her father writing it, swallowing his pride to ask for funds from a man whose wife he had stolen. She could sense some bitterness in it, too, in Robert Marsh's reluctance to care for a child that was not his own, left to him by a woman who had deceived him. But the letter had obviously never reached this Sir Jeremy Stafford. Since the baby girl had died, there was no reason to send it, so it was locked away to remain merely as evidence that Robert Marsh had been prepared to act honorably in this matter at least.

Alfreda sat thoughtfully for a moment, turning this new knowledge over in her mind and absently looking through the rest of the papers, which turned out to be nothing more than a few forever unpaid bills. These she discarded, but the letters she wrapped carefully in a handkerchief, along with the locket, and placed the bundle in her half-packed case.

As she finished organizing all the things she would be bringing with her, she began to form an idea of going to see this Sir Jeremy Stafford. Perhaps he would be grateful for the locket—grateful enough to help her find employment. She tossed the idea back and forth in her head, also thinking of all the arguments against it—he might be dead, he might be bitter about the past and have no desire to be reminded of it once more—but the more she thought about it, the more appealing the idea became.

She knew absolutely no one in England. Her only plan was to go to one of the agencies designed to find suitable positions for such as her, as a schoolmistress or governess in a respectable home. She was certain she had the proper qualifications—some teaching experience and a fluency in French and familiarity with French history and literature—but she was also aware that suitable positions did not come up every day and it helped to know someone with a certain amount of influence. She had adequate references from the parents of the French children she had taught—but would they hold any weight in England?

On the other hand, if she went to see Sir Jeremy Stafford, he might give her the opening she desired. It was a faint hope, but it would give her a sense of security to know that she had an object, a definite destination. She might even obtain a position in Sir Jeremy's own household; after all, it was possible he had remarried and had more children. This last did not seem very likely to her, though, for she imagined him to be quite old—now that her memory had been jogged, she could recall the unpleasant Caroline's references to an "old stick-in-the-mud," which she assumed meant Sir Jeremy.

Thus, scarcely realizing she had done so, Alfie made her decision. And if Sir Jeremy Stafford were unable—or refused—to help her, she could still carry out her original plan of going to a London agency. In some ways her father's daughter, she liked to have as many cards up her sleeve as possible.

Her shopping expedition the next day was a happy one. She felt lighthearted and purchased several cheap and cheery summer prints, which might not be exactly suitable for her intended role as governess, but which matched her present mood. Her best bargain was a cotton velvet in a rich emerald green. The material had a slight flaw, which Alfie could easily disguise, and this reduced the price of the goods to within her means. She started stitching immediately in order to have a new traveling suit ready for her voyage. With no more pupils to take up her time, the outfit was completed quickly and it became her more than anything she had owned since their prosperous days. The green of the material brought out the green in her eyes, and she arranged her dark thick hair in the latest Paris style, parted in the middle with a few loose ringlets framing her face. A new straw bonnet trimmed ingeniously with scraps topped off the ensemble and Alfie was eager to start her journey, feeling younger and prettier than she had for years.

The journey itself was uneventful, except for one incident while she was crossing the Channel that seemed unimportant at the time. She was sitting on the tiny deck, gazing at the sea, thinking very hard about what she would say to Sir Jeremy Stafford when she met him. She had run through a dozen possible conversations already when a slim and dashing young Frenchman approached her.

"So young to be thinking so hard, *madomoiselle*, he said, coming to stand beside her at the rail.

Alfie looked up and laughed lightly. "Hardly young, sir," she replied. "I'm all of five and twenty."

The Frenchman looked genuinely surprised. "I beg your pardon, *madame*. I took you to be eighteen at the most." He made a few more commonplace remarks and then left her side rather abruptly, for he had obviously not reached the quarter-century mark himself.

Alfie merely smiled at him and took it to be another effusive French compliment, of which she had had her share years ago, but she thought about it again as she sat in her tiny cabin later that evening. She did indeed look younger than her years, she thought, contemplating her image in a small hand mirror. She still looked very much the same as she had when she was eighteen or nineteen, perhaps even better, for she was more poised, more sure of herself now than she had been at nineteen. Her complexion was clear and bright, having lost its adolescent tendency to spot occasionally, and the excitement of returning to England and entering a new life had put a joyful and youthful sparkle in her eyes.

As she examined her face, a new idea began to take shape in her mind, an idea she was almost afraid of for its brilliance and boldness. She put the mirror down and opened her case, reaching in to find the letters she had so carefully laid away. She pulled them out and immediately found the one she wanted—the letter from her father to Sir Jeremy Stafford. A glance at the date and a quick mental sum determined that Miss Stafford, had she lived, would now be seventeen years old.

Alfreda took up the mirror again. Could she? Dare she? The mirror seemed to give her support. She thought of the new dress in her case, which was nearly finished. Perhaps with a ruffle of the same material around the neckline and the shoulders raised just a bit, it could be turned into a dress more suitable for a young girl of seventeen, who had not yet been presented to Society.

But dare she? A thousand jumbled thoughts ran through her head as she weighed the alternatives. The possibility of a teaching position did not seem very exciting when compared to the possibility of passing as the daughter of a baronet. The thought of actually reliving her youth, attending balls and wearing beautiful gowns once more, was infinitely preferable to setting up a school and spending the rest of her life at hard work.

Yet she knew it was not honest. Would her conscience leave her alone if she took this step? Well, she could make it up to her conscience. She would be an ideal daughter to the old and most probably ailing Sir Jeremy. She would sit quietly by his side in the evenings, make his tea, read to him.

This thought completed the decision. She knew Sir Jeremy had a large library—it was one of the constant though barely remembered complaints of the simpering Caroline. Even in her short letter she had mentioned that Sir Jeremy valued his books, and Alfie remembered the rest of Caroline's epithet for him: "old stick-in-the-mud with his nose in a book." It had left an impression on Alfie because even at the age of eight, she had loved reading and books, and she couldn't understand how that unpleasant woman could have spoken in such tones about something she herself held so dear.

Books—hundreds and hundreds of them she could imagine, as in some of the homes of wealthy Frenchmen she had once visited. The choice was made—she *would* do it. Who would ever know? Perhaps she would have the opportunity to fall in love and marry, as she had always dreamed.

She took up the letters that were still in her lap and replaced them carefully in her case, taking out instead the muslin print dress that was partly finished. She found a scrap of leftover material and held it to the bodice to see it if would fit in and raise the neckline to a more demure level, befitting a much younger girl than herself.

5

ARTHUR Huxtable waited nervously in Colonel Jennings' imposing library. The Colonel's evidence of having served in India was everywhere, for instead of books, the numerous shelves were lined with figurines of every description—bronze dancing girls and elaborate chariots, clay figures of women laden with jewelry, crude representations of strange animals, and other odd personages sporting many more arms than was decent. To the tutored eye, the collection was undoubtedly impressive, but to Arthur, it was merely horrible—every statue had its gaze fixed on him. The largest piece was a fat, laughing Buddha with piercing red eyes that occupied a place of some prominence on a shelf behind the desk. It was obviously a valuable piece, but Arthur would have gladly smashed it to bits, for he was certain the grinning statue was watching him with great amusement as he paced around the room, chewing on a fingernail now and then.

The door behind him opened and Arthur turned to face Colonel Arnold Jennings. Despite the fact that Arthur had been making himself familiar in the Jennings household for the past month and had enjoyed numerous chats with the head of that household, he felt ill at ease, like a schoolboy who has been called in to speak to the master.

"I'm sorry to have kept you waiting, Mr. Huxtable." Colonel Jennings held out his hand. He, too, sensed a difference in this interview and had adopted his most professional demeanor.

Arthur wiped his own hand quickly on his trousers before offering it to the suddenly imposing and stately Colonel. The fact that there was a slight smear of ink on Colonel Jennings' right hand nearly undid poor Arthur, for while he had noticed it many times before, Sir Jeremy's name for the Colonel now returned to him with new emphasis.

"Won't you have a seat," his host offered. Unfortunately, Arthur was forced to choose a seat directly opposite the mocking red-eyed god, who seemed to view his discomfiture with mischievous glee, noting every manifestation of his uneasiness. A painful pause ensued, as Arthur suppressed the almost overwhelming desire to call Colonel Jennings "Inky Arnold" and tried to think how he might begin his suit.

"I admire—"

"You wished to—"

These were both spoken at once, and Colonel Jennings bowed his head graciously to indicate that Arthur should speak first.

Arthur swallowed the lump in his throat. "I admire your daughter very much, sir."

"My daughter?" Colonel Jennings asked. He was not without a sense of humor, and while he knew perfectly well what Arthur was about, he would give him no help.

"Your daughter, sir." Arthur coughed slightly. "Your daughter, Miss Jennings, sir."

Colonel Jennings looked at Arthur as if ready to say something of profound importance. "Mr. Huxtable, I have five daughters, all of whom are named Miss Jennings."

"Your daughter, Miss Mary Ellen Jennings, sir."

"Ah." The sound was of sudden enlightenment. "Mary Ellen. Yes, Mr. Huxtable, I believe I have a daughter of that name. And what of her?"

"I—I admire her, sir."

"So you have said."

"I admire her very much, sir. In fact, sir, if I may be so bold, I am very fond of her."

"Indeed!" Colonel Jennings emitted this with great force.

Arthur tried to look everywhere but at Colonel Jennings. No matter how hard he tried, though, he could not remove the red-eyed god from his field of vision without turning his back completely, which would be terribly rude. He took a breath, with the air of one who is about to jump into icy water.

"Yes, sir," he said. "If you will pardon my further boldness, I would say that I love your daughter, sir."

"My daughter—?" Colonel Jennings gave an impression of genuine confusion.

"Your daughter Mary Ellen, sir."

"Well! And what of this love, Mr. Huxtable?"

Arthur was certain the red-eyed god's grin had widened. "I would very much appreciate it, sir, if you could see your way clear to giving me your daughter's hand in—er —holy matrimony, as it were." He felt relieved now that that piece of business was finally over with.

"My daughter—?"

"Your daughter Mary Ellen, sir."

Colonel Jennings leaned back in his seat, pondering this interesting prospect. "Now, let me see if I have this straight," he said. "You wish to marry my daughter."

"Your daughter Mary Ellen, sir," Arthur put in.

"My daughter Mary Ellen. Tell me—how are you situated?" This he knew well enough, but it was his duty at this point to inquire more exactly.

"Comfortable enough, sir," Arthur said, feeling more at ease. "We have a small house in London and a reasonably yearly income."

"We?"

"My mother and I, sir."

"I see. And you wish to introduce Mary Ellen to this house and mother?"

"Something like that, sir."

"I see." There was a long pause as Colonel Jennings seemed to weigh his decision carefully. Arthur's palms began to sweat even harder and the red-eyed god grinned and winked.

"Well," Colonel Jennings said at last, "I see no objections to this proposal. We must, of course, consult with my daughter—my daughter Mary Ellen, that is."

"Yes, sir! Thank you, sir!" Arthur rose and held out his hand, which was shaken firmly despite its dampness. Colonel Jennings then opened the door and three little girls of assorted sizes tumbled into the room, giggling as they bumped into each other. A fourth, larger girl still stood—she hadn't been leaning on the door herself.

"Girls!" Colonel Jennings boomed with all the force of the voice that had led men into battle against the Afghans. The girls all stood to attention, suppressing a stray giggle here and there. "Fetch your sister, Mary Ellen," was the command, and the four of them ran off down the hall, shouting, "He's asked! He's asked!" as they ran.

Colonel Jennings turned to Arthur. "You must excuse my daughters, they have an excess of youthful spirit."

The four messengers quickly returned with their eldest sister, who was blushing and smiling.

"My dear," Colonel Jennings said as she entered the room, "Mr. Huxtable wishes to marry you. I have given my consent, do you give yours?"

Mary Ellen blushed the harder. "Indeed, Father." She cast a shy glance at Arthur. "Indeed, Father. Indeed, Mr. Huxtable." She could say no more.

Colonel Jennings took over. "My dear Mr. Huxtable, as I believe my daughter means that she accepts your offer, may I be the first to welcome you into our family." He held out his hand to Arthur, and as they repeated this gesture for the third time, a cheer came up from the hall. Colonel Jennings smiled for the first time.

"I believe that means my family approves as well," he said.

While this touching scene was taking place, Sir Jeremy Stafford was sitting in his comfortable chair in his comfortable study, his feet on the desk, engrossed in a new book. Unfortunately, the book was not engrossing enough to prevent his occasionally losing interest and indulging in his own daydreams, which were much more exciting. It was while he was thus indulging that he fell off into a light slumber.

He was awakened sometime later by a discreet cough from Wilson, the butler, who had entered the room when there was no answer to his knock.

Sir Jeremy opened his eyes lazily. "Yes, Wilson, what is it?"

"Sir Jeremy, a young lady is here to see you. She would not give her name and she says it's important and rather personal, sir."

Sir Jeremy took his feet off the desk and sat up. "Did you mean a young *lady*, Wilson?"

Wilson understood the emphasis. "Yes, sir, a young lady, from what I can see."

"Well! And alone?"

"Yes, sir, quite alone."

"How did she come?"

"Dobson's cart, sir."

Sir Jeremy closed his book, which was still in his lap, and placed it on the desk. "Well, show her in, Wilson, show her in."

"Very good, sir."

Wilson reappeared in a few minutes, followed by a young girl in a fresh muslin print dress and straw bonnet, her hair pulled back demurely. Her eyes were wide with what might have been nervousness or excitement and she appeared to be quite young. Sir Jeremy stood up as she entered, regarding her with interest.

"How do you do," he said, bowing slightly.

"How do you do," she replied, returning with a curtsy.

There was a slight pause as they looked each other over carefully.

"Will you be needing anything, sir?" Wilson asked.

Sir Jeremy turned away from the girl and glanced at Wilson, whose presence he had nearly forgotten. "No, that will be all, Wilson." Left alone, he turned back to the girl, indeed finding it difficult to do otherwise for he seemed to be drawn to her.

"Won't you sit down."

"Thank you," she said, smiling shyly. "You *are* Sir Jeremy Stafford?"

"That is correct."

"Your father's name was Jeremy, too?" She seemed to be confused about something.

"No—I'm the first Jeremy in the family." He sat on the edge of his desk and folded his arms, a smile playing on his lips. He was already enjoying the interview, although he didn't know what it was leading to.

"You must forgive me," the girl said. "It's just that I was expecting a much older man than you seem to be."

"I hope you're not disappointed."

"Oh, no—just a bit puzzled."

"No more than I am, Miss—?"

Her eyes suddenly sparkled as she looked at him intently. "Sir Jeremy, that is exactly what I have come here about."

Sir Jeremy's eyebrows puckered. "I don't understand."

Alfie's heart was thumping wildly. The moment had come. She thought for the last time of giving her idea up and just asking for help in obtaining a job, but she swallowed the great lump that was forming in her throat and screwed up her courage. "Sir Jeremy," she said, barely loud enough to be heard, "I have reason to believe that you are my"—she was finding it difficult to come right out with it—"or rather, that I am your—daughter."

Sir Jeremy was certain he had not heard correctly. "I beg your pardon?"

Alfie took a deep breath and began her story as she had rehearsed it so many times in the mail coach from Dover. "My father—that is to say, my stepfather—died a month ago."

"Your stepfather?" Sir Jeremy interrupted, raising an eyebrow.

Alfie glanced away nervously. "I suppose he wasn't my stepfather, or any relation at all, but until a very short time ago, I thought he was my real father."

"But now you have discovered otherwise?" He gave her a quizzical look as he waited for the rest of what would undoubtedly be a very interesting story.

"His name was Robert Marsh," Alfie said. "I suppose you must have heard of him because he ran off—"

"Yes, I know who he was," Sir Jeremy said shortly.

Alfie continued. "Before he died he told me that I was not actually his daughter. That my mother—whom I never knew—had been married to someone else and was already expecting her child when my—when Robert Marsh brought her to France. He told me that my real father was Sir Jeremy Stafford. When he died, I had nowhere else to go and no one to turn to, so I thought I had best come here and make myself known to you." She glanced uncertainly at Sir Jeremy to see what his reaction might be.

He was looking at her with an expression of distinct amusement. "A very touching story," he said, "and how fortunate for you that you might provide yourself with the happy ending of restoring the long-lost daughter to the bosom of her family." His tone was frankly sarcastic.

Alfie felt a spark of anger stir within her. She had expected a certain amount of skepticism, but not this mocking reception of her story. "Sir Jeremy, let me assure you, I was as astonished as you must be when I learned the truth. As I said, Robert Marsh always led me to believe that I was his own daughter."

Sir Jeremy said in a cold voice, "And let me assure you that I am not astonished at the truth because I have not yet been convinced of it. I must say I am more astonished that you should expect me to believe this fairy tale. I was assured by reputable sources that my daughter died in infancy, and until you furnish me with adequate proof to the contrary, I will not accept you or anyone else as that daughter."

"I don't blame you for feeling that way," Alfie said. "After all, anyone in possession of the facts might come here and pose as your daughter." She felt rather smug as she noticed the expression on Sir Jeremy's face that indicated he was about to make the same observation. "I can only tell you what I know to be the truth," she went on, "and hope that you will believe me. I was born on November 25, and I will be eighteen on my next birthday. If your sources told you the date of the birth of your daughter I think you will agree that it would be too much of a coincidence were I not that daughter."

Only a little of the coldness had left Sir Jeremy's voice. "It certainly would be a coincidence, if indeed that is your birthday."

"I see you will be hard to convince, Sir Jeremy," Alfie said with a rueful smile.

"If I were as gullible as you seem to think me, I'm sure this house would be swarming with young women, all claiming to be my daughter. If each of them presented such a story as you have, I would be hard put to decide which was telling the truth." He gave a small involuntary shudder as he imagined vividly the condition his words had described. "I don't suppose you have anything so out of the way as a birth certificate?"

"I'm afraid not," she replied, undaunted. "I don't believe they were required."

"No, I didn't think so." He was not surprised by her answer. "There is one thing that puzzles me, though. Why should Robert Marsh raise you, if indeed he did, if you were not his own child? I never knew the man well, but he didn't seem to be a particularly charitable sort of fellow."

Alfie faltered. She had not expected a question of this nature. "I—I don't know. Perhaps he was lonely. He had lost his wife and then my mother died and—well, he was alone in a strange country." But even as she said it she realized it sounded rather feeble.

A smile twisted Sir Jeremy's mouth. "It seems to me that a man in his position would prefer, shall we say, a more mature female to assuage his loneliness. And why did he wait until he was on his deathbed to tell you who you really were? You will pardon my saying so, but I cannot help but notice that your dress is not exactly of the first quality. If you even knew Robert Marsh, did he strike you as the sort of man who would want to saddle himself with the responsibility of raising a daughter when he could barely afford to clothe her properly?"

Alfie raised her chin proudly and looked Sir Jeremy straight in the eye. "I did indeed know Robert Marsh and he had a great deal of kindness—certainly more than you credit him with. But I don't blame you for having a feeling against him, Sir Jeremy. After all he did run off with your wife. But all I can say is he raised me as a daughter—why, I cannot tell you, but it was a fact."

Sir Jeremy returned her gaze, and unknown to both, there was something strangely alike in those two pairs of eyes. It was not in the color or the shape, but in the directness and clarity and even fierceness of the way they regarded each other. Perhaps Sir Jeremy did realize something of this, for suddenly Alfie reminded him of his mother, who had been the only other person in his life who could outstare him.

He suddenly chuckled. "Well, though you are not my daughter, you must have inherited someone's habit of looking down your nose that way." In spite of himself he felt a liking for this girl. His tone was kinder when he said, "Forgive me, but unless you have something more to tell me, I really must ask you to leave. I appreciate the circumstances that may have led you to attempt this little charade, but you must realize that I can claim no responsibility for you. Surely you must have some genuine relatives who will care for you. I will even help you to go to them if you wish." He had no idea why he was making this offer, for as he had just said, he had no responsibility to her, but she looked so young and vulnerable, and while she might be a bold-faced liar, she was still obviously gently bred and should not be allowed to travel alone.

"I am sorry, Sir Jeremy, but *you* are the only relative I know of. And I do not wish to leave just yet, for as it happens I have a great deal more to tell you." Alfie spoke this briskly, heartened by his sudden softening. "You wondered why Robert Marsh did not tell me earlier of my true identity. I'm afraid I cannot answer that question, but I do know that he had considered sending me to you at first."

Sir Jeremy was alert. "How do you know that?"

"I have here a letter written by him shortly after my birth. It was never posted—but here, you can see for yourself what he says." Alfie held out the letter to him and he took it from her wordlessly. He read through it quickly and then looked again at Alfie.

"This is dated November 28, 1825."

"That is correct," Alfie said. "Three days after I was born."

"Where did you find this?" Sir Jeremy's voice was sharp again, not as before from disbelief, but because he was suddenly being forced into reluctant belief.

"It was in a strongbox of my father's—I mean, my stepfather's."

Sir Jeremy looked the letter over carefully. His first thought was that it might be a forgery, but he realized almost immediately that this could not be so. For one thing, the paper had yellowed with age and the crease where it had been folded was very delicate and liable to tear with any rough handling. He knew those conditions could be artfully devised, but what would be the point with a letter of this sort? If she wanted to forge herself indisputable proof that she was his daughter, surely it would be of a more straightforward nature. This letter left one important question unanswered—why had it not been posted so that Sir Jeremy could comply with the request, as he would have willingly? Why had Robert Marsh decided to raise her as his own daughter? Was it spite or genuine affection? But somehow the answers to these questions were unimportant compared to the fact that the document did indeed give credence to this girl's claim to be his own flesh and blood.

All these thoughts ran quickly through Sir Jeremy's mind, and when he looked up, he saw Alfie was holding something else out to him.

"This was with the letter," she said, holding the locket by the chain so that it twisted and twinkled with the light from the window.

Even as Sir Jeremy stood up to take it from her he knew what it was.

"I'm sorry it's been dented," Alfie said. "But the key to the strongbox was lost and I had to force it open. In the process, I'm afraid the locket was damaged."

Sir Jeremy sank back into his chair, as if his legs had turned to jelly. This was all so sudden, he needed time to think. He opened the locket slowly, afraid lest the ghost of Caroline lurked within, ready to leap out and haunt him. And indeed it did. There was the picture just as he remembered, the golden hair, the clear blue eyes, the classic regularity of the features. It had been done at his request, one of the few requests his wife had willingly granted, for she was as fond of her own likeness as any man in her life had been. In a sort of daze, Sir Jeremy tore his gaze from the delicately painted miniature and looked up at the girl who sat patiently awaiting his reply.

Was this, indeed, the product of his marriage with the stunning Caroline, whose likeness he now beheld for the first time in nearly eighteen years? There didn't seem to be much resemblance. The girl was beautiful, he thought, but not in the same glittering, hard way as Caroline had been. In fact, there seemed to be little likeness at all between this girl and the Caroline he remembered, but then children didn't always take after their mothers. And if she was an imposter, how could she have produced two such pieces of evidence? Admittedly, the locket could have come from a French pawn shop, but it certainly would not have been accompanied by the letter.

Alfie was trying to ignore Sir Jeremy's stare by examining the room around her. If Sir Jeremy himself had been rather unexpected, being much younger and indeed more handsome than she would have supposed, here at least was exactly what she had hoped for—books, hundreds of them. And most of them she had probably not read since her experience had been mainly with French literature and the English classics. She smiled with sheer delight at the treasures she might find within.

Sir Jeremy finally broke the silence. "You are smiling?"

Alfie could not hide her pleasure. "It's all these books, Sir Jeremy. I've rarely seen so many in one place."

"Do you enjoy reading?"

"Oh yes!" she said, her eyes shining.

"Then you obviously do not take after your mother in that respect, I am most happy to say." He held the locket on the end of his finger and swung it back and forth. "She and I had very little in common."

Alfie did not miss the implication of that statement and she smiled even more broadly in her triumph.

"Yes," Sir Jeremy said with some amusement, "I am prepared to believe that you are, indeed, my daughter. I asked for proof and you have very obligingly presented it. And—why, I'm afraid I've forgotten to ask your Christian name."

"Alfreda," she replied. "Although I'm usually called Alfie."

"Alfie," he repeated, trying out the sound of it, "Well, Alfie, it seems I must keep you here and we must make up for seventeen years of separation."

"I look forward to that, Sir Jeremy."

He halted his swinging motion for a moment. "You must cease this 'Sir Jeremy' business, you know. I suppose you should call me Papa or Father or something else equally appropriate."

Alfie grinned. "You seem too young to be called Papa."

"Do I? Well, I was very young when I married, and I must say I don't feel as if I'm ready to pack it in yet. But as to this problem of nomenclature—what did you call Robert Marsh?"

"I called him Father," Alfie said, almost apologetically.

"I see. Well, that wouldn't do for me then. And it wouldn't do for you to call me Jeremy either, since you needs must show proper respect for your elders. I don't know—perhaps we had best leave it at Sir Jeremy for now until one of us comes up with something more suitable." This decision relieved them both, for Sir Jeremy was not too fond of being reminded of his advancing years by having this nearly grown up woman's call him Father, and Alfie thought him much too young to be her father were her true age known.

The two looked at each other again, both instinctively liking what they saw. Alfie found herself wondering what might have happened if she had met him five or six years ago, as herself. Somehow she felt her life would have been very different. Already she felt as if she had met a kindred spirit. While he had been quite abrupt with her at first, she had expected no different, and indeed would have thought less of him had he not questioned her story carefully. Somehow she felt they would find they had a great deal in common.

Sir Jeremy, thinking similar thoughts, which were leading him to the almost reluctant conclusion that this was indeed his daughter, suddenly forced himself into action by placing the locket on the desk and standing up. "I suppose we should have you settled in. You must be tired from your journey, so why don't you have tea in your room and rest a bit. Then we can decide what to do with you over dinner. I'll ring for Wilson."

But before he could reach the bell pull the door burst open and Arthur Huxtable came in, breathless and beaming.

"Jerry, I have been made the happiest of men. Mary Ellen Jennings will marry me." He suddenly noticed Alfie, and giving a slight bow, said, "Oh, excuse me, I didn't know you had company, Jer."

Sir Jeremy smiled. "It seems to be our lucky day, Hux. You have gained a wife and I a daughter. Allow me to present Miss Alfreda Stafford. Alfie, this is my old friend, Arthur Huxtable."

6

$\mathscr{A}$RTHUR Huxtable could not close his gaping mouth for several moments. Sir Jeremy took the pause in the conversation as an opportunity to ring for Wilson. Arthur barely had time to collect himself and say how do you do to the unexpected Miss Stafford before Wilson was at the door—his usual quick efficiency enhanced by his curiosity over who this lady might be.

"Ah, Wilson," Sir Jeremy said, "this is my daughter, Alfreda. She's come back to live with us, so would you kindly show her to her room."

Wilson's impeccable training prevented him from reacting as violently as Arthur Huxtable had, although he was certainly just as surprised. He merely said, with his usual decorum, "Very good, Sir Jeremy. The green room?"

Sir Jeremy nodded, inwardly admiring Wilson's restraint. He turned to Alfie, "We dine at seven. That should give you enough time to settle in and rest from your journey."

Alfie smiled. "Thank you, Sir Jeremy." She held out her hand to Arthur Huxtable. "My congratulations to you, Mr. Huxtable." With that she gave a pretty little curtsy and followed Wilson out the door.

When they had gone, Arthur turned to Sir Jeremy. "Jer! What—? Who—? You could have knocked me down with a thingummy." With this he fell back into the chair vacated by the lately discovered Miss Stafford, a look of amazement on his face.

Sir Jeremy offered him a cigar, which he weakly refused; his response was more enthusiastic to a glass of brandy. After a few swallows, he was again able to speak. "I must say you seem to be taking this remarkably well, Jeremy."

"Or you're taking it remarkably badly," Sir Jeremy replied, seating himself behind his desk once more.

"Are you sure—is she really?"

"She has represented herself as such and I see no major reason to disbelieve her story. She presented me with a locket containing the fair Caroline's image and a letter from Robert Marsh to me. Here it is," he said, pushing the letter across the desk to within Arthur's reach. Arthur, however, was still more interested in his brandy and didn't bother to pick the letter up. Sir Jeremy continued. "It seems he was asking for money to send my daughter to me when she was only a few days old, but as the letter was never sent, he obviously reconsidered."

"Eh? Oh yes, you're right, of course," said Arthur, who wasn't listening very carefully and to whom the name Robert Marsh meant nothing, but he sensed that some reply was required. He took another swig of brandy. "What a day, first I must come up to scratch with the old man and then I learn that my best friend has been a father for—how many years?—and didn't even know it."

Sir Jeremy gave a lazy smile. "Seventeen. Do you think you can handle it, Hux?"

"You might at least have given me warning," Arthur said petulantly.

"Warning? When you burst through the door without so much as a knock?"

"Sorry, Jer, I was a bit excited."

Sir Jeremy's faint smile spread a little wider. "I believe I have yet to offer my congratulations, Hux. I wish you and Miss Jennings the greatest happiness."

"Thank you, Jer, thank you." Arthur was looking very pink and pleased, partly because of the brandy and partly because of all the excitement.

Sir Jeremy puckered his eyebrows for a moment. "But, Hux, if you are now engaged to the charming Mary Ellen, what are you doing here? Shouldn't you be there, paying court?"

"Had to come back to change for dinner," Arthur said reasonably, as if it were the most natural thing in the world to travel ten miles in each direction to change for dinner.

Sir Jeremy threw back his head and laughed. "You *are* in love, Hux. How many times have you sat down to dinner here in your riding clothes, all stained and spotted with mud? I declare, I'm quite jealous."

Arthur merely took another swig of brandy in reply. "So this daughter of yours—quite a beauty, eh?"

Sir Jeremy looked thoughtful. "Yes, but not in the same way as Caroline was. She seems to take after my side of the family."

"I suppose so," said Arthur, "although she don't resemble any of your sister's cubs. I'll have to take a better look, of course, but she seems to have your eyes."

"Do you think so? They aren't the same color, of course. Actually, she reminded me more of my mother than myself. It's very strange," he said thoughtfully, "but I liked her the minute I saw her, before she told me who she was. I felt there was a certain—affinity, I suppose—between us. Although I didn't believe her story at the first, I still had the sense that if we were both in a crowd of people, we might have singled each other out."

"Well, that's not strange if she's your daughter, Jer," said Arthur. "And I don't think anyone would have any trouble picking either of you out in a crowd—I mean, she has your height." He finished off his brandy and gave a deep sigh. "What are you going to do with her?"

"I haven't quite decided yet. I expect we'll give her a Season. My sister should like that, she always wanted a daughter to dress up and show off and all she had was four sons. It's a bit late in the year to launch her now, but I'm sure she'll keep until spring. Meanwhile, I suppose I'll just keep her here and get used to the idea of being a father." Sir Jeremy reached over his desk for the letter from Robert Marsh to place it in the drawer, but before he laid the locket to rest on top, he opened it once more and studied the picture.

Arthur looked on with interest. "What's that?"

"The image of the fair Caroline, my onetime wife," Sir Jeremy said, a note of bitterness in his tone. He handed the locket to Arthur, who took it eagerly, anxious to see what kind of wife his friend had once chosen.

"She certainly was a beautiful woman, Jer. It's no wonder—"

"No, it wasn't any wonder. She was beautiful and I was young, foolish, and infatuated."

Arthur examined the face again. "You're right, Jer, your daughter—what is her name again?"

"Alfreda."

"Alfreda don't take after her mother, from what I can see. Coloring's all wrong."

"I'm glad she doesn't, Hux," Sir Jeremy said, taking the locket back. "I don't think I could bear it if she looked like Caroline."

Arthur shook his head sympathetically. "May be just the thing for you, Jeremy. I've always thought you needed a woman's touch around Stafford Hall. I had a wife more in mind, but I suppose a daughter would do just as well."

"Perhaps she won't be here very long, though."

Arthur looked at him quickly. "Eh? What do you mean?"

Sir Jeremy smiled. "Oh, nothing sinister, Hux. It's just that with her looks and my money, she'll most probably be married halfway through her first Season."

Arthur chuckled. "Cecily ought to enjoy that."

"Yes," Sir Jeremy agreed. "I must write to her immediately and tell her of her newfound niece."

"Don't forget to add in my bit of news. We may be able to save putting an announcement in the newspaper if we just tell Cess."

"Yes, and it would probably be a more efficient way of spreading the news, too," Sir Jeremy replied.

Alfie started trembling as she left the library to follow Wilson up the stairs to her room. The great danger was over, Sir Jeremy had accepted her story. But while she had been calm and composed throughout the interview, she could not prevent her knees from quaking now. It was after the event that she began to think of all the things that might have gone wrong—things she hadn't allowed herself to think of before, questions he might have asked for which she had no answers prepared, or a slip of the tongue revealing information she was too young to know. Fortunately, nothing *had* gone wrong, unless she counted the fact that Sir Jeremy was too attractive and too young to fit in with her cozy image of reading to him by the fireside.

The strain of the journey suddenly hit her, and she felt very, very tired, glad for the opportunity to have a quiet tea and take a short nap before dinner. Wilson opened a door at the end of a long hallway, indicating that she should precede him into the room. It was a large and airy bedroom, with wallpaper speckled with tiny flowers, white lace on the curtains and bed, and a deep green carpet from which it received its title. It had been a long time since Alfie had slept in such elegant surroundings and she began to feel refreshed already. Wilson stepped in behind her, placing her case on the floor.

"Shall I have your tea brought up now, Miss Stafford?" he asked, enjoying the novelty of saying her name.

"Yes, please, Wilson."

"Will you be sending for your trunks, Miss Stafford?"

"My trunks?" She laughed. "I'm afraid I have no trunks—this bag is all my luggage."

Wilson nodded. "Very good, Miss Stafford. I shall send Hawkins up to you with a tray."

"Thank you, Wilson."

Wilson nodded again and left, closing the door carefully behind him even though he wished to get downstairs as quickly as possible to tell the news of Alfie's arrival to the rest of the staff.

Left alone, Alfie took her bonnet off and tossed it on a chair. She then went to the window, and pulling aside the curtain, was afforded her first good look at Stafford Hall's grounds. The scene was peaceful and lovely—from her window she could see part of the formal gardens, colorful with midsummer blossoms. She could also catch a glimpse of the stable and paddock beside it where a few horses were contentedly feeding, and a bit of what must be the kitchen garden. In the distance the hills rolled away lush and green, dotted with cottages and a silver thread of water.

Yes, Alfie thought, this was worth any amount of scheming and lying. She felt she could be truly happy here, for this was the England she remembered from her childhood and had longed for ever since. She turned away from the view and noticed how comfortable and inviting the bed looked. She didn't think it would hurt to lie down for a few minutes before the maid brought her tea, and before she knew it she was fast asleep with all her clothes on.

Alfie was awakened several hours later by a knock on the door. She gave a faint "Come in" and a bustling, capable looking woman entered and immediately started speaking.

"Welcome home, miss," she said. "I'm Hawkins and Wilson told me I'm to look after you. I'm sorry you missed your tea, but you didn't answer when I came with it, so I thought it best for you to have your nap. *Surely* you haven't gone to sleep with all your clothes on? I can see already where you take after your father—absent-minded and all. I must tell you, miss, it was quite a surprise to us downstairs when Wilson gave us the news of your arrival. It was as if we had all been struck dumb at one and the same time. A few of us here knew your mother, deary, although I was no older than you are now at the time. I must say, you don't seem to take after her, and that's a blessing. No offense intended, of course, though you never knew her yourself, but it might have been a trial to Sir Jeremy if you had walked in looking like your mother's ghost. Of course, you couldn't have a nicer, kinder father if you were allowed to choose him yourself, and as it is, we're all very glad to have you here. It's been too long since Stafford Hall has seen a mistress. Lady Stafford, your grandmother, died more than twenty years ago, and your mother wasn't here long enough to make much of an impression. My word! You don't seem to have any evening dresses!"

During this speech Hawkins had been undressing and bathing Alfreda as if she were a doll. This last remark was made when she opened Alfie's case and shook out the three dresses that were in it. One was the green traveling suit; the other two were poor, dark dresses from Alfie's teaching days, which she had saved out of necessity.

"Well!" said Hawkins. "It seems you'll have to put that little muslin on again, though it's hardly proper for dinner at Stafford Hall. I see you have some lengths of cloth in here. We'll have to see about having them made up for you. You must speak to your father about this, deary."

Alfie smiled. "I'm afraid we couldn't afford much in Paris. I never needed an evening dress there."

"Well, you're at Stafford Hall now, where you belong." Hawkins helped Alfie into the muslin dress she had been wearing before, after shaking it vigorously to remove the traces of its use as a nightgown. After fastening the dress, Hawkins expertly arranged Alfie's hair in a style perfectly becoming to a seventeen-year-old.

"Ah, miss," she said, "it's a pleasure indeed to have a young lady to look after. I always wanted to be a lady's maid, but there hasn't been much chance for that here. I looked after your mother for a short time, but she never had any patience with me, I was such a clumsy young girl then."

At last Alfie was dressed and, although not exactly in proper evening attire, she looked very young and fresh. She felt her fears return to her, though, at the prospect of continuing her masquerade at dinner; but the look in her eyes could as easily be taken for excitement at her new surroundings as a fear of disclosure. Besides, she told herself, this was just the first night and she would have to become used to playing her part if she hoped to remain undisclosed.

Sir Jeremy rose as Alfie entered the drawing room. He felt very peculiar as he watched her give a little curtsy. This is my daughter, he thought, my *daughter*. Though he had been trying to convince himself of this fact all afternoon, it would take more time for him to really accept it. Meanwhile, he would assume his new role one bit at a time.

"I see we must furnish you with a new wardrobe," he said, noticing she was wearing the dress she had arrived in. "Your present one seems rather limited."

"Forgive my appearance, Sir Jeremy. Actually, Hawkins was quite outraged."

"No need to apologize." He held out his arm. "We're

dining alone this evening, I'm glad to say. Mr. Huxtable
has returned to the side of his betrothed. We will have a
chance to get better acquainted."

Alfreda smiled shyly. Her heart was pounding as she
took Sir Jeremy's arm and entered the dining room.

Their conversation at dinner was centered on Alfie's
life in Paris. Sir Jeremy was interested in finding out how
she had been raised, and while she told him the truth
mainly, she was careful to omit the last eight years or so
of her life. Sir Jeremy had never been to France himself,
he had lost all desire to travel when he lost his wife, so
Alfie's descriptions of Paris were new and entertaining to
him.

"So," he said finally, as the meal was finished, "Robert
Marsh died of drink."

"Yes," Alfie said, casting her eyes down. The look in
his eyes disturbed her for some reason and she suddenly
realized it was because it reminded her of herself. How
often had she seen or felt that same look in her own eyes,
a look of defiance mingled with anger and pain, the chal-
lenge to fate to do its worst because, although hurt, she
would not be beaten. She had felt it when she watched
her father fall deeper and deeper into debt and drink. She
had felt it when, in recent years, she had seen the gay
and lovely Parisian ladies going to another ball, knowing
that she had once been among them and should be still if
only her father's luck had held. And now she saw the
same look in Sir Jeremy's eyes, as he learned that his
supposed daughter had spent her life with a drunkard,
too poor to buy her a proper evening dress.

"Why so pensive?" Sir Jeremy's tone was soft.

Alfie spoke the truth. "That look in your eyes when you

spoke of my stepfather. It was a look I recognized in myself."

"How interesting," Sir Jeremy said, looking into her eyes more carefully than before. "Hux mentioned that you had my eyes, but you don't, of course—they're quite different. I noticed it earlier—it's the expression that's the same. You gaze right through a person as if searching for his innermost thoughts, in a manner for which I am famous." He smiled suddenly. "But I hope that in time we'll discover we have more in common than an imperious stare. As for now, why don't I show you over the house? You have a bit of catching up to do on the family history."

Alfie welcomed this suggestion for she had become a bit uncomfortable under what Sir Jeremy referred to as his imperious stare. "Yes, that would be lovely," she said. "I noticed some traditional family portraits lining the halls upstairs, but I didn't have a chance to see anything closely."

Sir Jeremy chuckled as he rose from his chair. "I don't think the family portraits deserve more than a cursory glance. I'm afraid they're not very good—most of them were done by itinerant painters. Too close a look would lead one to believe that either my—*our*—forebears were exceedingly ugly or the painters exceedingly bad. And I must say, I'm inclined to believe the latter, out of personal conceit if nothing else."

Alfie laughed warmly as she rose and took his arm. Their tour did not take very long, since the house was not overly large. Because the Stafford name and holdings were older than the title, the house had been built for a country squire with utility rather than ornamentation in mind. Few alterations had been made since it was built

three hundred years before, and there was a simplicity—
almost a spareness—in the dimensions of the rooms that
was very pleasing. The great entrance hall was impressive,
with a large oak staircase leading to the first floor and
great oak beams that had been left uncovered instead of
plastered and papered over as in some of the smaller
rooms. But these rooms, too, although modernized and
quite tastefully decorated, provided a kind of family history, for each seemed to have been redone in a different
period and the styles of decorations, furnishings and
painted ceilings gave a nearly accurate timetable of the
increase in the Stafford fortunes. Sir Jeremy was obviously
proud of the house, and while many of the bedrooms were
unused, they did not seem forbidding but were kept in
good order. The whole house seemed inviting and warm
in the flickering candlelight and Alfie fell in love with it
immediately.

They completed their tour back in the drawing room,
where Sir Jeremy indicated the small piano that stood in
the corner.

"Do you play?" he asked.

"Not to speak of," Alfie replied. "I wouldn't want to
be called upon to play at a party, but I used to do a bit
for my own enjoyment."

"Would you do some for my enjoyment?" Sir Jeremy
requested.

"Certainly, if you can bear it." She laughed, taking her
place behind the instrument.

Sir Jeremy settled himself in a comfortable chair to
listen. "I'm afraid you'll find it out of tune," he apologized.
"I don't play myself."

Alfie proceeded to play a few French airs, which comprised most of her repertoire. After she had exhausted what she knew by heart, which took only about fifteen minutes, she stopped and closed the lid.

"Not only is the piano out of tune, but I'm out of practice," she said.

"Never mind, come and sit down."

Obediently, Alfie took a seat on the sofa opposite Sir Jeremy.

He smiled. "We shall send you up to my sister's soon, so you can be outfitted properly. I believe it's a bit late in the Season to present you, though—we will wait until next year for that."

She smiled back at him, amazed that he had already made plans for her future. "That would be fine, Sir Jeremy. It will give me a chance to do some reading and accustom myself to England."

He questioned her about what authors she enjoyed reading and a lively literary discussion ensued. Sir Jeremy was impressed with her knowledge of French literature, although she seemed to have read little of the popular British authors. She was eager to hear his recommendations in this area, and he was just as willing to offer them. He took her into his study, pointing out books she might be interested in, giving her some off the shelves to take up to her room.

It was late when they finally retired for the night, Alfie going to her room with her arms laden with Dickens, Scott, and Austen, the fruits of their search. Sir Jeremy could not remember the last time he had spent such a pleasant evening, and as he walked up the stairs to his bedroom, he felt strangely happy and content. He was still unable to accept completely the fact that this nearly grown-up woman was his daughter, but as he had told Arthur Huxtable, he knew that if she had been no relation to him at all, he would have liked her just as well.

7

*L*ADY Chandler sat at the breakfast table, surrounded by her husband and her two eldest sons, John and Geoffrey. Even at this early hour she looked very elegant in a turquoise morning gown that reflected the blue of her eyes—eyes very like those of her brother. She had been a beauty in her youth, but instead of trying to retain the traces of her girlish beauty as so many other women unsuccessfully attempted to, she had decided to grow old gracefully and elegantly. She was certainly not averse to employing some artificial assistance, but she applied her cosmetics with a skillful hand, enhancing her strong points rather than covering up her weak ones. Of course, her still youthful vitality and joy in living went a long way toward making her one of the most attractive matrons in London.

The family were eating their breakfast in silence as Lady Chandler went through her daily routine of arranging the morning post into neat little piles—a pile for invitations, a pile for letters requiring immediate reply, including those from her two younger sons at school containing urgent requests for funds, a pile for letters requiring no reply, and a pile for bills. Occasionally, she sent an envelope sailing across the table to her husband at the other end, often just barely missing his tea. Long practice on Lord Chandler's part, however, prevented such a disaster from ever occurring.

"Well, upon my soul!" Lady Chandler exclaimed suddenly. "Here's a letter from Jeremy. I don't believe he's written to me since his first week at Eton."

The regular routine was halted while Lady Chandler tore open Sir Jeremy's letter and read it quickly. She gasped at several points, and when she was finished, she noticed that her family was waiting expectantly.

"What do you suppose, Richard," she said, not unaware of the drama of the situation and eager to make the most of it.

"I'm sure I have no idea, m'dear," Lord Chandler replied.

"Jeremy's daughter has arrived at Stafford Hall." The announcement was made with all the importance it deserved.

"I didn't know he had a daughter," Lord Chandler said, a trifle confused.

"That's exactly the point! Neither did I—neither did he, to be sure. We were all led to believe that she had died as an infant."

Lord Chandler began to catch on. "But she didn't?"

"Apparently not, for she showed up at Stafford Hall just the other day."

"I say." Lord Chandler was properly amazed.

Lady Chandler turned her attention back to the letter. "It seems she was unaware of her identity until Robert Marsh died a month ago."

"Robert Marsh?" Lord Chandler was lost again.

"The odious man who ran off with Caroline, Richard."

"Ah, yes." Lord Chandler replied as if he understood perfectly now, although if he had ever heard the name before, he certainly didn't recall it.

"It also seems," Lady Chandler continued, "that she will be paying us a visit shortly in order to buy new clothes and see London."

"How very nice," said Lord Chandler. He was genuinely pleased, for like his wife, he had always wished for a daughter, though he was certainly not disappointed in his four sons. "It will be pleasant to have a fresh young face around the place. How old did you say she was?"

"He doesn't say here, but I suppose she must be—oh," Lady Chandler did some quick mental arithmetic—"at least seventeen," she finished finally.

"Seventeen? A bit too old to play with George and Jason, then."

Lady Chandler smiled slightly. "Yes, I should think so, Richard. She must be quite a young lady now." Suddenly her eyes sparkled as she realized the implications of this. "Why, we'll be able to give her a regular Season. How lovely. We'll have a big ball to present her and I'll invite every eligible bachelor in England. She'll need lots of new gowns, too. Oh, I do hope she isn't plain. I shouldn't like to feel like all those poor mamas who practically beg me to ask John or Geoffrey to dance with their daughters just so they won't go into a decline."

The two young men thus referred to had been listening to the conversation with interest and here exchanged sympathetic glances.

"Well, m'dear," Lord Chandler said, "I'm sure you'll have plenty of time to make your plans. After all, won't you have to wait until next spring?"

"Yes, of course, but Jeremy wants me to take her shopping immediately, and as long as she'll be staying with us, I don't think a small card party would be out of order."

"Whatever you think best, m'dear," Lord Chandler said. His wife's social plans did not much concern him, for even if she asked for his assistance or advice, he knew how to render these things in such a manner that he was told to get out of the way completely—which, indeed, was what he did best.

Lady Chandler glanced at the letter one last time before folding it up to be placed on the proper pile. "Oh, Richard, here's something else. Arthur Huxtable is to marry that sweet little Mary Ellen Jennings."

"Hux getting married, eh?" Lord Chandler said. "Now that *is* news."

As Sir Jeremy must have known she would, his sister wasted no time in spreading the word of his newfound daughter to most of London Society. Since he had not indicated the exact day of their arrival, Lady Chandler's plans were made all the more exciting by the small measure of uncertainty and her anticipation was heightened every day. She had the best guest room prepared for her niece and sent out invitations for a very small card party, appropriate for a young lady not yet out. As the days went by, though, and her brother and his daughter still had not arrived, she began to be concerned that the evening of the party would arrive without a guest of honor.

Sir Jeremy gave as the excuse for the delay the affairs of the estate, but it was actually a desire to keep Alfie to himself for a few extra days. He found he enjoyed her company more than that of any woman he had ever known, for unlike them Alfie was not constantly trying to flirt with him, displaying all her charms to gain a new necklace or some other trinket, or possibly even to trap him into marriage. He was able to converse with her as an equal on any number of subjects, for while her knowledge of certain things was limited because of her uneven education, she had very decided opinions on most matters nonetheless. Sir Jeremy liked it even more when these opinions differed with his own, for a heated discussion of a kind he had not enjoyed since his university days would then ensue. However, while he was reluctant to break up the new and delightful routine of his days, the constant reminder at dinnertime of Alfie's pitifully small wardrobe convinced him he must make the trip to London.

Alfie enjoyed the ride immensely. She had come up from Dover in the mail coach, which would have afforded only an imperfect view of the English countryside even if she had been lucky enough to gain a window seat. In Sir Jeremy's well-sprung and spacious coach, Alfie was able to view the passing landscape much more easily. She asked constant questions of Sir Jeremy, exclaiming when she recognized a name from her reading, and he answered with a patience that would have surprised Arthur Huxtable, telling her tales of historical events that had occurred in the places they traveled through.

They arrived in London in good time and found Lady Chandler awaiting them eagerly.

"My dear Jeremy," she began before they'd stepped through the door, "you might have been more definite about when you were coming. We've all been at sixes and sevens for the past few days, wondering when you'd arrive."

"My apologies, Cess," Sir Jeremy said, more out of habit than courtesy. "May I present my daughter, Alfreda."

"Alfreda," Lady Chandler said, tasting the sound of that name. Alfie dropped a shy curtsy, uncertain of what she should reply. Lady Chandler continued, "We are all so happy to have you here. But we'll have plenty of time to get acquainted later and right now I'm sure you would like to freshen up, so I'll have Stuart show you to your room. I understand we have a great deal of shopping to do. We can start this afternoon if you are not too tired."

Alfie assured Lady Chandler that she was not too tired, and secretly thought that she had little choice in the matter, so she obediently followed the said Stuart upstairs to her room.

As soon as Alfie was out of earshot, Lady Chandler turned to Sir Jeremy. "Now, Jeremy——"

"I'm afraid you'll find me more difficult to get out of the way than my daughter, Cess."

She laughed. "I assure you, Jeremy, I have no desire to get you out of the way. On the contrary, you must tell me all about this charming daughter of yours. Come into the parlor and have a drink of something."

"Thank you, Mrs. Spider, said Mr. Fly," Sir Jeremy said as he followed her into that room.

"Richard will be so disappointed that he missed your arrival," Lady Chandler remarked after Sir Jeremy had been provided for. "He's been so looking forward to meeting her."

Sir Jeremy smiled his faint, lazy smile. "I'm glad Alfreda is finding such a warm welcome here."

"Alfreda—what a dreadful name. Imagine the nerve of that woman giving your child such a name." Lady Chandler looked properly disgusted.

"I'm sure she didn't stop to consider your feelings, Cess—nor mine, for that matter. But you'd have taken exception to her name if it were Cecily."

"She wouldn't have the audacity to name her daughter after me—not when she treated our family in such a despicable way. But tell me, Jeremy, is she quite nice? She hasn't been brought up in bad ways, has she?"

Sir Jeremy had no trouble sorting out his sister's pronouns, for he was used to her way of jumping willy-nilly from one thought to the next. "I assure you, Cess, Alfie's conduct is everything you would wish it to be, but that you shall shortly see for yourself."

"Ah, yes," Lady Chandler said dreamily. "I have so many things planned for her. It will be quite wonderful to have a niece to take around, almost as if she were my own daughter. I've already sent out invitations for a card party Tuesday night, and I thought a small picnic might be in order, if the weather allows. And we can take her to the theater, if you think it's quite proper. Of course, I don't know what she was used to in Paris, but I'm certain whatever we can offer in the way of amusements will be more than adequate."

"Don't plan too much, Cess. I intend to take her back to Stafford Hall as soon as she has some clothes. Most likely she'll stay only a week or so."

"Jeremy!" Lady Chandler stood up, outraged. "You

don't mean to incarcerate her in Stafford Hall until the next Season begins? Why, the poor girl will die of ennui. Besides, it's so unfair to snatch her from me just when I've been telling you of all the things I've planned. It's positively selfish of you."

"Cecily, your excesses of temper give me a headache." He took a sip of his drink, as if to stop that malady. "I intend to return to Stafford Hall with my daughter, where we shall remain until the spring. The reason for this is very simple. Since I have little doubt that she will be married before the end of the next season, this will be the only opportunity I will have to play father in my own home, as it were. Perhaps I am being selfish, but in this instance I feel I have a right to be."

Lady Chandler was somewhat mollified. "When you put it that way, I suppose I can see your point."

Sir Jeremy smiled. "Speaking of marriages, what do you think of Arthur Huxtable's intended nuptials?"

Lady Chandler was immediately interested again, and forgot her very recent set-down. "Yes, isn't it wonderful! And to think they met at my ball." The contemplation of this fact was almost too much for her matchmaking heart, and she sighed contentedly.

"Perhaps they'll thank you at the ceremony," Sir Jeremy said.

Lady Chandler gave him a quelling glance. "When is it to take place?"

"Very shortly, as soon as Mrs. Jennings completely recovers from her accident."

"How lovely that will be. Why, Hux is almost part of the family. And the girl is a dear little thing. I think they shall get on splendidly."

Lady Chandler desired to know more details, of which

Sir Jeremy had none. Realizing that there was no more to be gained from that quarter, she resolved to pay a call on Mrs. Huxtable in the near future. In the meantime, her attention would rest on the pressing problem of dressing her niece. The already delightful prospect of being able to spend as much of her brother's money as she desired was enhanced by the wonderful opportunity to dress someone from the skin out, as it were, something she had not done since she used to make gowns and petticoats for her dolls when she was small. Lady Chandler had a marvelous sense of style and the outing promised to be a well-favored one.

Alfie was no less enthusiastic, and the two women, starting out on such ground, got along famously. Lady Chandler was impressed by Alfie's stylistic insights, believing her to have a knowledge of clothing far beyond her tender years, but this she attributed to her having lived in Paris. Alfie was trying her best to behave innocently, realizing how easily she might give herself away as several times she prevented herself from exclaiming that a certain gown or cloth reminded her of a dress she had worn six years before. She bravely checked her taste for the more flamboyant styles, expressing a preference for more demure frocks and paler colors—a preference she did not really feel. But her youthful delight with the London shops was genuine, and after quieting the pricks of her conscience at spending so much undeserved money, she quite enjoyed herself as they purchased more clothes than she had ever owned at one time, even in her father's best years. Lady Chandler insisted on the best quality everywhere they went and Alfie found herself being measured for everything from dainty petticoats to promenade dresses to pink and white evening gowns.

They arrived home barely in time to change for dinner, having taken tea quickly between shops. Alfie was glad to know that this would be the last time she needed to wear the simple muslin dress in the evening, as some of the things they had ordered would be delivered the very next day.

At the dinner table Alfie met several other members of her new family, her uncle and her cousin Geoffrey. Lord Chandler she liked immediately, as he shook her hand warmly and welcomed her.

"You must excuse my not being here when you arrived, m'dear," he said, "but Jeremy does enjoy surprising one." He lowered his voice slightly and said with a confidential wink, "Glad you've finally made it, there's been no living with Cecily since she received your father's letter. You trot her around and tire her out and things will be more peaceful."

Alfie returned his smile. "I'll certainly do my best."

"So, Jeremy," Lord Chandler said, turning to him, "things must be getting dull for you down at Stafford. I've a notion you've been hiding this girl down there and just popped her out for a bit of excitement."

Sir Jeremy smiled slightly. "How did you guess? It was selfishness, you see—I've been keeping her to myself all these years just so I could educate her properly and keep her away from corrupting influences. It was an experiment of sorts."

"Oh, what nonsense you both speak," Lady Chandler put in. "Why, Alfie's been telling me all day about Paris— she was quite helpful, too, for she was able to tell me the latest Paris fashions. She'll be more up to date than any girl in London."

"Too unfortunately true," Sir Jeremy said. "Not that

Alfie will be up to date, Cess, but that she's been in Paris when she belonged here. I feel that I've been cheated of her company for all this time."

"Amen," Geoffrey Chandler said, just loud enough for Alfie to hear. He was on her right side and she noticed very quickly that he was paying a great deal of attention to her. He had been somewhat sulky earlier when his mother asked him to dine at home in order to entertain his cousin; further annoyed when he found that his older brother, John, had been allowed to dine out. His disappointment disappeared, however, upon his first sight of Alfie and he spent the rest of the evening making himself agreeable to her. This occupation consisted mainly of passing the butter or salt to her before anyone else had a chance to do so—and usually before she had asked for it—and looking at her longingly.

Alfie could not help but feel amused by this young man, five years her junior. She remembered many similar attentions from the Frenchmen she had once known— the only difference being that either the Frenchmen had been better at it or Alfie was now too old to be affected by such nonsense.

Lady Chandler noticed Geoffrey's behavior, too, and wasn't sure she approved. She liked Alfie, but thought her son much too young to be thinking seriously of any girl, especially when she thought of the mistake her brother had made. Alfie seemed too mature for Geoffrey somehow, most likely because of her unnatural upbringing. Why, exposure to French ways was bad for anyone, let alone a young, susceptible girl. She decided she would let Geoffrey continue in his attentions only because there was nothing she could do about it immediately, but if his feelings seemed to progress, Lady Chandler would certainly speak to him about them.

When they had finished their dinner, the two ladies arose to retire to the drawing room.

"Oh, Jeremy," Lady Chandler said, pausing at the door. "Will you be spending the week here or at your club?"

"I will be returning to Stafford tomorrow. What would I find to do in London for an entire week? I can't think of anything more boring."

Alfie was dismayed by this piece of news, for she, too, had counted on Sir Jeremy's spending the week in London.

"What about tonight, then?" Lady Chandler asked.

"My club, I think," Sir Jeremy replied.

"Very well," said Lady Chandler complacently, for this was the answer she had expected and had made no preparations for her brother, though it was her duty to inquire. She and Alfie retired to the drawing room, but Alfie found it difficult to converse with Lady Chandler for she was tired out from a long day spent traveling and shopping. She was disappointed, too, that Sir Jeremy would be leaving her here—she had wanted to show off her new clothes to him and generally share his company as she had done for the past week.

"You look quite done in, my dear," Lady Chandler finally said. "I've been keeping you up with my chatter. You've had a full day, why don't you go straight up to bed?"

Alfie smiled. "Yes, spending money is an exhausting occupation, but I thought I might just wait until I had a chance to say good night to—to Sir Jeremy." She could not bring herself to say "my father."

As it was, she had not long to wait, for Sir Jeremy, too,

was tired and the men had not lingered long over their brandy. It was an unsatisfactory farewell for Alfie, with none of the familiarity that she and Sir Jeremy had come to enjoy, but she was comforted by his promise that he would be back to fetch her in a week. A week wasn't so very long, after all, and there would be so much for her to see and do in London. Alfie went to sleep happy and content with her lot in life, even though she had cheated a bit in the drawing.

8

$\mathcal{I}$T promised to be a busy and exciting week for Alfie. Although she missed Sir Jeremy, there were so many things for her to do and see that she barely had time to notice his absence. She and Lady Chandler spent nearly the whole of the next day shopping again, this time to buy all the things they had forgotten the day before, such as gloves and ribbons and lacy handkerchiefs. With all her new and beautiful gowns, styled for a girl of seventeen, Alfie found it quite easy to look and act as young as she was supposed to be.

But while her part became easier to play each day, Alfie was finding it very hard to keep her overactive conscience in line. She couldn't even begin to add up all the money that had been spent on her in the last two days, but she knew the amount was staggering. Worse than the money, though, was the fact that she had been taken into this family's confidence and was being given their unquestioning love and affection. Alfie was not reluctant to return this feeling in kind, and she had been lonely too long not to appreciate it, but she knew it was undeserved. If Sir Jeremy and Lady Chandler learned of her true identity, they would be horrified at her perfidy and would have every right to turn her into the streets without a penny. A hundred times a day Alfie decided to ease her conscience, disclose all, and leave them with no more than a distasteful memory, but just as often she thought of the gowns, the comfortable beds, the security, and most of all that pained, tired look in Sir Jeremy's eyes—the look that she knew in herself—and she could not leave. His heart had been broken once before by an inconstant woman and Alfie did not wish to be the agent of any further heartbreak. If she remained, perhaps she could bring him some happiness and that look would fade in time—from both Sir Jeremy's eyes and her own. Besides, now that she was already in so deep, it was much the easier path to go along with the deception she had begun. Alfie was enjoying her new life, she liked Lady Chandler and her family, and she had already become too attached to Stafford Hall and all it represented to give it up so easily.

She soon found that Lady and Lord Chandler had many evening engagements that could not be broken and that she was not permitted to attend, having not yet been properly introduced to Society. Far from being lonely, Alfie made good use of the time to catch up on her reading of books she had heard of or books Sir Jeremy had recommended. One evening, Alfie had the whole big house to herself, the servants excepted, while Lord and Lady

Chandler were at a ball and John and Geoffrey off pursuing their own interests. The Chandlers' library was not so extensive as Sir Jeremy's, but Alfie was able to find an interesting book to curl up with in a comfortable chair.

After she had been thus pleasantly occupied for about an hour, the door opened slightly and Geoffrey Chandler poked his head in.

"I say, it's too bad of them to leave you here all by yourself like this," he said when he saw Alfie.

She looked up and smiled. "Oh, I don't mind. In fact I quite enjoy being left alone now and then."

If this was meant as a hint, Geoffrey did not take it as such. Instead he came in and sat down near Alfie. "You might be saying that to be polite, but I think it's a silly way to spend your time."

"You don't care for reading?" Alfie asked, hiding her amusement.

"I suppose it's all right in its way, when it's not something deadly dull like what they made you read in school— but there are so many better things to do. Of course, *you* can't do anything, not being presented. That seems a trifle unfair to me, too—why, a person has to run his life according to Society's timetable."

"A very profound observation, I must say"—Alfie closed her book for courtesy's sake—"although I understand it's for my benefit. It seems most of the eligible men have gone to the seaside by now and, after all, the whole business is just for eligible parties to meet one another."

"If you don't mind my saying so, you'd have no trouble finding someone if they presented you in the dead of winter." Geoffrey gave her an admiring glance.

"Thank you, Geoffrey," Alfie said. She tried to think of something polite to say that at the same time wouldn't encourage him. "I'm sure you've turned many girls' heads these past few months."

"I daresay." Geoffrey was not one to minimize his own attractions. "But I can't say any one of them compared with you."

"You're very kind," Alfie said, as flatly as she knew how. "Well, I'm feeling a bit done in, I think I'll be going up to bed."

"I didn't mean to keep you up, it's just that, Alfie—may I call you Alfie?"

"Of course, we're cousins, that's almost like brother and sister." This time the hint was stronger.

"Alfie, I wish you were staying more than just a week. It's rather selfish of my uncle to keep you all to himself."

"Don't worry, Geoffrey, we're family. I'm sure we'll be seeing more than enough of each other over the years." With that she took her leave of him, so she could continue her reading undisturbed in her own room.

At breakfast the next day, Lord Chandler suggested to his wife that she take Alfie on a small tour of London.

"I declare I would like that, Richard," Lady Chandler said, smiling, "but I'm afraid I'm a bit fatigued with two days of shopping and the ball last night. I must get caught up on some correspondence as well. Alfreda won't mind waiting until tomorrow, will you, my dear?"

Alfie acknowledged that this would be no inconvenience to her and she expressed concern for her aunt's state of health.

"I say, Mother," Geoffrey exclaimed, "why shouldn't *I* take Alfie about? I know all the places she might like to see."

Lady Chandler wished she could think of a good reason that he should not, but before she could reply, her husband said, "Why, that's a splendid idea, Geoffrey. Don't you think so, Cecily?" He turned to his wife.

Lady Chandler did not think so, but could not say as much without appearing unreasonable, so she merely replied, "Certainly, if Alfreda agrees."

Alfie thought it a splendid idea, too. She felt quite rested and would welcome another outing to keep her mind off her recurring attacks of conscience. Geoffrey would make a nice, if somewhat eager, companion, provided she continued to remind him that they were cousins.

Geoffrey himself could have crowed with delight. He immediately began rattling on about all the places Alfie would enjoy seeing, until his mother was ready to scream at the noise. When breakfast was over, Alfie ran upstairs to change from her light morning gown to something more suitable for traveling around London in an open carriage.

Lady Chandler was none too pleased as she saw them off. Geoffrey's cheery "See you at teatime, I hope" was not calculated to improve her temper, nor was Alfie's appearance, for she looked very smart in one of her new outfits, a walking dress of deep blue trimmed with white, with a small matching bonnet trimmed with a few perky white feathers. If Lady Chandler had but known of the sisterly affection Alfie held toward Geoffrey, she would have felt a great deal better. As it was, she turned to her husband as the two sightseers left, furious.

"Richard, how *could* you?"

Lord Chandler, who had been smiling happily at the pleasure of his son and niece, was taken aback. He looked at his wife in confusion. "M'dear, whatever do you mean?"

Lady Chandler sighed with exasperation. "Richard, don't you see? Geoffrey is too young for an involvement right now. He should wait a few years."

Lord Chandler laughed, an action that did not win his wife's approval. She glared at him all the harder and he said, "M'dear, Alfie seems to have her head attached the right way. I'm sure she can take care of Geoffrey, and besides, what could transpire on a harmless sightseeing tour?"

Lady Chandler was not comforted. "I can think of a great many things that might transpire! And it's certainly not Alfreda I'm worried about, it's Geoffrey. He's so *impressionable*. He's bound to say or do something improper and outrageous, like propose to her. And I don't believe in marriage between cousins, it's just not healthy. Look at the royal family of—"

"My dear Cecily," Lord Chandler interrupted, "you are taking things far too seriously. Why, they've hardly known each other for more than two days and in your mind you have them married with idiot children. Alfie will be returning to the country at the end of the week. Begin to worry when the next Season begins, when they'll be meeting each other regularly at balls, with Alfie looking her best in all the lovely gowns you two will choose for her."

"Richard," Lady Chandler said through her teeth, "it is not I who am taking things too seriously, but you who are not taking things seriously enough. You refuse to see past the end of your nose—if the house were burning down, you wouldn't notice until your feet caught fire!" With that she turned and left him standing in the hall, about to remark that his feet were a great deal farther away than his nose and thus there was a basic fallacy in her statement.

As it turned out, Lady Chandler needn't have worried. The pair arrived home in time for tea, with Geoffrey looking very sulky and Alfie very indignant. They seemed to be in the middle of a misunderstanding as they came in the door.

"I say," Geoffrey was saying, "I don't agree with your idea of what to see. If you wanted to spend all your time trotting around Westminster looking at dead kings in boxes, you should have asked Mrs. Lytton-Harshaw to take you about." Mrs. Lytton-Harshaw was a particularly garrulous old woman with a reputation for pushing social reform—she was not well liked by Geoffrey or any of his set.

Alfie was not to be outdone. "I have no idea who your Mrs. Little-whatever may be," she replied hotly, "but I do know that I have no interest in cock fighting, nor is a horse auction a place where I should be taken, I am sure."

The strains of this argument reached Lady Chandler where she sat at her desk, answering the mountains of correspondence she had. To her it was sweeter than music to hear them falling out, and in a much better humor than she had been in all day, she went down to greet the two sightseers.

"I say, Mother," Geoffrey said as she entered the hallway, "if I had known that all she wanted to see were some silly churches, I wouldn't have offered to take her about in the first place. I point out Westminster Abbey to her, just in passing, and the next thing I know she's stopped the carriage and says we're going in—and the same thing at St. Paul's. It's really too bad." With a final, pettish glance at Alfie, he stalked up to his room, leaving the two women alone.

Alfie smiled. "I'm afraid Geoffrey's and my ideas of seeing London differ somewhat. He seemed to take it rather hard."

Lady Chandler smiled back benevolently. "Don't worry, he's still a silly young boy. I'm glad you made it back in time for tea."

The rest of the week passed quickly for Alfie. Geoffrey grudgingly took her sightseeing one more time, at the insistence of his mother, although he did not hide his boredom at being forced to walk through museums to see musty old statues and faded paintings. The small card party that Lady Chandler had arranged was a success, although Alfie found it very hard to hold her tongue and play her supposed years. A dozen times she wished to set down half the silly young ladies she met, as well as their mothers, with a biting and clever remark. However, she controlled herself valiantly and even managed to learn a few new card games and gain a few new admirers. Unfortunately, Geoffrey's admiration for her had not been entirely squelched by her pedantic inclinations and he hung about her continually at the party, with the result that his mother did not enjoy her little affair as much as she should have. Her only consolation was that other young men had also gathered around Alfie. The attentions of all these admirers and the card game itself left little time for Geoffrey to advance his own suit with Alfie. Lady Chandler was almost sorry she liked Alfie as well as she did, for she would have enjoyed giving her niece a good talking to. Instead, she privately counted the days until her brother would be back to collect her.

Alfie, too, was counting the days. She missed Sir Jeremy more than she would have believed possible. She also missed Stafford Hall, where in such a short time she felt that she had come to belong. It was the perfect ending to the dream she had cherished for so long, for Stafford Hall reminded her of her own childhood home, very gracious, very spacious, and very English. The feeling of belonging there had come upon her quickly, but she hadn't realized how strong it was until she was taken away from it, and while she was enjoying her stay in London, the flighty attentions of her adopted cousin Geoffrey were beginning to irritate her. He was like a little puppy dog who wagged his tail when his mistress was kind to him and whined and sulked when she was not—and Alfie was finding it more and more difficult to be kind to him, especially since it was so much more peaceful when he was off sulking somewhere.

At last the much-awaited arrival of Sir Jeremy took place. Alfie found it hard to resist throwing herself into his arms, with less than—or more than, depending upon which way one looked at it—daughterly affection. He seemed pleased to see her, too, as she meekly curtsied to him in an unexceptionable manner.

His smile was warm. "You seem to be looking more fashionable than when I last saw you, Alfie," he said.

"I shouldn't want you to think your money was wasted, Jeremy," Lady Chandler put in.

Alfie hated to think just how wasted it really was, if her true identity were known. "Will we be going directly back to Stafford Hall?" she asked.

"Yes," Sir Jeremy replied, strangely pleased with her eagerness. "The county races are to be held in a week and then we have a wedding to attend fairly soon afterward. The bridegroom has taken Stafford Hall as his hotel and we can't leave him too long without a host— although he does spend most of his time at the Jennings'."

Lady Chandler beamed. "They're certainly not wasting any time, are they, Jeremy?"

"Once Hux gets an idea into his head, there's no

stopping him until he's seen it through. It's too bad he has so few good ideas." Sir Jeremy seated himself on the arm of a chair, but upon a frown from his sister moved to the seat. "I suppose we will be expecting all of you in about a month. I'm sure you won't want to miss the festivities."

"Certainly not!" Lady Chandler exclaimed. "We wouldn't miss it for anything. I'm looking forward to seeing Stafford again, too—you're very lax with your invitations, Jeremy."

"Cess, you know perfectly well I dislike entertaining. But you are welcome to come any time you like. After all, it was your home, too, at one time and I certainly wouldn't lock the doors against you."

"Be that as it may, Jeremy, I dislike visiting without a proper invitation. The few times I just turned up you made me feel—I won't say *unwelcome*, but certainly ignored. However"—here she adopted a more confidential tone—"I don't know if John will be coming with us. I wouldn't like to be premature, but it seems we might have another marriage soon—right in the family."

"All these weddings are giving me a headache," Sir Jeremy said. "Not that Stanley chit?"

"Jeremy! Arabella Stanley is an exemplary young woman, and an heiress, too."

"If there's anything I dislike more than an exemplary young woman, it's one with money," Sir Jeremy said in a philosophical tone.

"Jeremy, you're incorrigible," his sister said, with a disgusted snort. "The young lady is quite pleasant and I have no objections to having her as a daughter-in-law. But even if John can't tear himself away, the rest of us will be down at Stafford Hall several days before the wedding. The boys will be out on holiday by then and it will be a nice treat for them." She cast a glance at Alfie. "And I'm sure Geoffrey will be eager to come.

Sir Jeremy raised an eyebrow. His single "Oh?" was extremely expressive, and although Alfie thought she had forgotten how to blush years ago, she felt a red tinge creeping into her face at that moment. Sir Jeremy noticed this, and was not sure he cared for the implication.

"Well, one thing is certain," Lady Chandler said. "Alfreda has turned up at a very opportune time. I hesitate to think what your entertainment would be like at Stafford Hall without a mistress. I'm sure your daughter will fill that gap wonderfully."

Alfie was grateful for the change of subject and even more grateful for Sir Jeremy's sincere agreement with his sister. Perhaps their relationship would not be all one-sided, she thought to herself. She might not be able to read to him by the fireside of an evening, but perhaps whatever contributions she could make to the comfortable management of his home would repay his kindness to some degree. And playing hostess beside Sir Jeremy was not an unpleasant prospect in Alfie's mind.

9

ALFIE was glad to be once more back at Stafford Hall and once more in the company of Sir Jeremy. She had entertained him on the trip back with her first impressions of London, including Geoffrey's disapproval of her interests, and the journey had seemed very short indeed. Almost before she knew it, they were driving up the long graceful avenue to the estate and Alfie knew the warm feeling of homecoming. At the Chandlers' town house she had been a guest, but Stafford Hall was home—already she had become part of it and it part of her.

"Sure, miss," Hawkins said to her, helping her unpack the many boxes and trunks she had brought back, "we all missed you while you were gone. We were afraid they'd want to keep you up there, when we had the pleasure of your company for only a short time."

Alfie smiled. "I don't think I would have liked staying away any longer than I did," she said. "This is where I live, this is home to me."

"And from our view, too, miss. Why, the change in Sir Jeremy is something to warm the heart. Do you know that while you were gone, he set about making all sorts of little changes just for your pleasure?"

Alfie sat on the bed, crushing a beautiful gown in her arms. "Was he, Hawkins? Did he?"

"Here now, miss," Hawkins admonished, "you don't want to go putting all sorts of wrinkles in that." She took the dress from Alfie and shook it out vigorously. "My word, but each one is more lovely than the next. Stafford Hall will certainly be much brighter when you're parading around in these, miss."

Alfie giggled happily. "Must I parade, Hawkins? Can't I just walk, like anyone else?"

"Oh, go on with you, then," Hawkins said. "Here, this pink one will do for dinner tonight. Look at them ribbons, it's fair covered with them."

"You're worse than a mother would be, Hawkins, telling me what to wear and how to walk!" But while she pretended to pout, Alfie was enjoying it. She hadn't been fussed over since she was a small girl and her mother had dressed her lovingly in a brand new frock.

As instructed, she wore the pink dress down to dinner that evening and glowed all the more for Sir Jeremy's admiration. Indeed, he felt quite proud when he saw her, thinking over and over—still trying to convince himself—this is my daughter, *my* daughter. He smiled at her warmly and said, "When you first arrived I was afraid my quiet life here would be disturbed, but now I find the disturbance is a welcome one."

Alfie returned his smile brightly. "I think I have never been happier in my life," she said, secretly adding to herself, not even when I was six years old.

"I have been remiss in one thing," Sir Jeremy said as he led her to the dining room. "It seems that my tenants are very disappointed that I did not immediately take you on the grand tour of the estate so they could all meet you. They would like it, and so would I, if you accompanied me on my rounds one morning, so that we may make up that deficiency."

Alfie grinned. "I would very much like to, but if you expect me to ride, I'm afraid it would be impossible. I've never learned."

Sir Jeremy frowned. "That is a problem," he said. Of course, he thought to himself, I should have realized that. She had never yet suggested a ride, but he had attributed that to her lack of a riding habit rather than inability, since to him riding was as familiar and easy as walking. "We shall have to make up for that. I'll find you a nice, gentle horse and Jamie can begin teaching you immediately. Meanwhile, I can take you around in my curricle. We'll have to stick to the roads, of course, but at least you will be able to see something more of the countryside than you have yet observed from the windows of my coach."

"That will be nice," Alfie said, "and I will learn to ride as soon as I can, especially since we purchased a rather expensive riding habit that I was afraid might not see any use. However, Lady Chandler would not hear a negative response to any of her suggestions when we were shopping."

"I certainly wouldn't want my money to be ill spent," Sir Jeremy said, smiling again. Alfie felt the now familiar twinge of her conscience at his words. Why, she thought to herself, was I not born as unscrupulous as my father?

As good as his word, Sir Jeremy had his curricle ready the next morning for Alfie's "grand tour." She was impressed by the size and beauty of all that he owned. Perhaps it was, not so vast as the lands of some of the peers in the county, but to Alfie it seemed like an entire kingdom, with Sir Jeremy as the king, of course. And since he took an active interest in the running of his estate, everything was in good repair and all the most modern farming techniques were used to the mutual benefit of Sir Jeremy and the farmers who worked his land. Alfie could tell when they came to Stafford's boundaries, for suddenly the fences looked a bit shakier, the hedges were not so neatly trimmed, and there were stones missing from the stiles. When she pointed this out to him, he was justifiably proud in his reply that those who didn't care for the land should not be allowed to own it. Of course, some of his neighbors thought Sir Jeremy overly concerned, which perhaps he was, but he had found that land, unlike people, returned as much or more than it received and was therefore one of the few things he trusted completely.

Alfie enjoyed her outing, but when Sir Jeremy offered to drive her out again until she could ride with him, she demurred. While she felt he had enjoyed her company, she also felt that driving slowed him down too much. He had a great deal to see to—or a great deal he felt he ought to see to—and it was much easier for him to go on horseback. He was therefore a bit relieved at her refusal and promised her that as soon as he obtained a suitable mount, her lessons would begin.

Unfortunately, there was nothing in the stable for a

beginner. Most of Sir Jeremy's horses were high-strung
racing animals or carriage horses. But after a few days he
purchased a gentle gray gelding, almost as old as Alfie
pretended to be, which had not been known to go above
a trot in its life. But that was just as well, from Alfie's
point of view, since the only horse she had ever been on
in her life was a diminutive pony when she was six years
old. Even the gelding's sedate pace seemed terrifyingly
swift to her and she was in constant fear of falling from
the great height of its back.

Jamie was given the duty of instructing her, and while
he was more used to working with high-bred stock and
experienced riders, he was very patient as he showed Alfie
how to mount, how to dismount, how to sit, how to hold
the reins, how to start the horse, how to stop the horse,
and how to turn the horse. Alfie grasped the concepts
quickly, but in practice she caused the poor horse much
confusion by kicking him and pulling on the reins at the
same time. When she at last succeeded in making him
walk, she would pull on the reins again in order not to
fall off, and the horse would stop once more. When she
had gone through this process at least three times, with
Jamie explaining each time what the trouble was, she
heard a long laugh coming from the path leading to the
house.

She looked up in some embarrassment to see Sir
Jeremy watching her with amusement. "Well may you
laugh," she shouted to him hotly, "you've been riding all
your life." In her annoyance she inadvertently delivered
an unnecessarily hard kick to the side of the horse who,
obediently, took off in the fastest trot he had managed in
some years. Alfie was terrified and lost her hold of the
reins, hanging onto the saddle for dear life. Fortunately,

the horse's pace, although his best, would certainly not be called excessive, and Sir Jeremy ran to him easily and caught him by the bridle. He looked up into Alfie's frightened face, barely suppressing his laughter.

Alfie was more angry with herself for being so foolish than with Sir Jeremy for laughing as she said to him coldly, "I'm sorry to have disappointed you, but it seems I will never make a good rider." She thought about dismounting, but the distance to the ground seemed greater than ever. Sir Jeremy noticed her intent, and letting go of the bridle, he reached up and took her by the waist, lifting her down as if she weighed no more than a bird.

He set her down in front of him, his hands still on her waist. Alfie felt her heart pound wildly at his touch and, her anger gone, she looked into his eyes. He, too, seemed suddenly serious and his gaze was direct as he seemed to search her face, seeking her innermost thoughts. Alfie, suddenly remembering who she was supposed to be, tore herself out of his grasp, her face burning. With an inarticulate sound she turned and ran to the house, longing for nothing more than the comfort of her own room where she could quiet her racing pulse and compose herself.

Sir Jeremy watched her as she ran off. He was transfixed for a moment, confused by what had happened, and most of all, confused by what he had seen in Alfie's eyes. His reverie was broken when a soft, damp nose touched him on the back of the neck. He recollected himself, took the horse by the bridle, and led him back to Jamie, who had been watching the whole scene with interest and no small amusement.

"Well, Sir Jeremy," Jamie said when his master was within earshot, "if the old gray's too much for her, I don't know what we'll do."

Sir Jeremy smiled. "Give her time, Jamie. After all, it's her first time on a horse."

"Well, sir," Jamie said with an answering grin, "we'll see if we can't make a rider out of her yet. And since she's your daughter, I shouldn't think it would be too hard."

"I certainly hope not, Jamie, and she did get more speed out of this fellow than I've ever seen. But let's put the old man away and look at some of the livelier stock. I noticed the black seemed to be favoring his right hind leg a bit—perhaps we should tape it up. I don't want any of my horses running lame in the races tomorrow."

The examination and admiration of the racing horses was a prospect delightful to them both and Sir Jeremy soon forgot the little incident, for the moment at least.

Alfie, once she had composed herself, determined that she would not give Sir Jeremy further opportunity to laugh at her efforts. Indeed, it seemed the very next day she improved a great deal. Jamie was not present to give her his valuable instruction, since he had gone to the races with Sir Jeremy, but under the guidance of one of the younger stable hands, she practiced what she had been told the day before until she had it right.

She was a fast learner, and after she recovered from her initial fear of falling off, it became easy to apply all that Jamie had told her. From a desire to please Sir Jeremy, Alfie spent almost three hours practicing, wearing out the horse as well as herself. She was not surprised to find that her muscles were stiff and sore that evening— while she was riding she had felt no pain at all, but when she came down to dinner her legs were suddenly unwilling to do as she bade them. She walked stiffly into the drawing room and sat down, waiting for Sir Jeremy before going into dinner.

She had not spoken to him since the incident of the day before—he had been gone all this day and had had an engagement for dinner the evening before with a solicitor in a nearby town. Arthur Huxtable had dined at the Jennings' as usual and her meal had been lonely, but she was grateful for it. She wasn't really certain what she should say to Sir Jeremy. She hoped fervently that he had not noticed the thumping of her heart, or that he had attributed it to her narrow escape on the horse. She suddenly smiled at the thought of having a "narrow escape" from the old gray's ambling gait, feeling much more confident after her successful lesson of that morning.

Sir Jeremy entered to find her still smiling to herself. "You are looking cheerful this evening," he said. "I understand you had another lesson today, which went more successfully."

"Yes," she said, trying to rise. She gave a wince of pain and fell back into her comfortable chair.

Sir Jeremy laughed. "Perhaps it wasn't too successful from that point of view. You'll soon find it easier, though. You'll be able to ride for hours without feeling it at all." He walked over to assist her out of the chair and into the dining room.

"I hope that day comes soon," Alfie said. "I feel as if all my muscles have rebelled against me and are refusing to do as I request." Especially my heart, she thought ruefully as that organ started its unnecessarily strong thumping at Sir Jeremy's touch. I am his daughter, I am his daughter, she repeated over and over to herself as they entered the dining room, but it was difficult to remember that, for she liked him better than any man she had ever met. She almost laughed at herself for all the silly young Frenchmen she might have married, had she been allowed. How boring it would have been for her, she now realized. She never would have been able to live this life of deceit, which was much more exciting than her truthful French life had been. But actually, she thought, she was more able to be herself with Sir Jeremy—all of those charming French suitors of her youth would have been at a loss if she engaged in a literary discussion with them, or even if she had said anything more intelligent than "La, sir, you turn my head." Perhaps Sir Jeremy was different only because he didn't try to flirt with her but spoke to her as an intellectual equal, not as someone whose head was filled with cotton wool. She could feel justified in her deceit when she was able to make him laugh, in a way which he himself admitted he had not enjoyed in years.

Tonight, however, the atmosphere was a bit strained. The memory of what had passed between them the day before was still strong in both their minds. Alfie had given little thought to anything else since, and she longed to know what Sir Jeremy was thinking when he occasionally treated her to the same searching glance that had transfixed her yesterday. She asked him how his horses had run, and attempted to entertain him with tales of new progress on horseback, but while he replied suitably and even became quite expansive in his description of how the black horse had won its race by six lengths, underneath there was a current of thoughts and feelings held back.

"I see we shall soon have to buy you a more suitable mount," Sir Jeremy said, after a silence that ended his description of the final race. "Jamie seems to think you have a natural seat, and that you only want a bit of practice and confidence to make an excellent horsewoman."

Alfie glowed at the praise. "I certainly value Jamie's opinion," she said. "He was so patient with me. But after my display yesterday, I thought he would never want to see me on horseback again. It must be very boring for him to bother with someone as inexperienced as I am."

"I wouldn't worry about that," Sir Jeremy said, smiling his strange crooked smile. "Everyone at Stafford Hall is delighted to have you here. They have needed a mistress and you are fulfilling their needs more than adequately."

Alfie lowered her eyes. "I am trying, Sir Jeremy. I suppose I've been so used to the idea that one must earn one's keep that I really feel as if I'm not doing enough. If there are any small duties I could do for you—?" She looked up at him once more.

"For me, it's enough to have you here. It's not only Stafford Hall itself that has missed the influence of a mistress—I was becoming too much of a recluse. In a few more years I might not even have been human any longer. But as to doing anything else, once you are more comfortable on horseback, you can take hot soup and baskets of goodies to the farms. I remember my mother used to do that when I was young. It seemed there was always some sick child who needed special attention, and their mothers were always so grateful to have something special to tempt them back to health."

Alfie smiled again. "Well, they'll have quite a laugh for themselves when they see me jogging along, clinging to the horse with all the grace of an elephant."

"Come, I have more faith in you than that." Sir Jeremy arose. "But now I've a notion to teach you to play chess. I was thinking the other day that it would be a pleasant way to while away the evenings. I used to be quite proficient at it and I believe you'd make a worthy opponent."

Alfie stood to follow him to the drawing room. "Thank you for the compliment, sir, she said, though I won't vouch for the equilibrium of my knights. But you know, Sir Jeremy, I'm quite miffed. You haven't asked me to entertain you on the piano since my first night here. One would think you didn't appreciate my musical talents."

Sir Jeremy laughed as he began to set out the chess pieces. "I didn't want to offend you, but if you think you'd like to practice, I'll have someone come in and tune it for you."

"That might be nice. I shall become what Miss Austen refers to as an 'accomplished woman' with all these new pursuits."

10

$\mathcal{I}$NDEED, as the weeks went by, Alfie found more and more things to keep her busy at Stafford Hall. Soon her soreness from riding disappeared and she began to enjoy her lessons more. Sir Jeremy kept his promise of a new mount by providing her with a lovely bay mare, which Alfie found a bit frisky at first, but a much more satisfying horse than the old gray. She then found new pleasure in riding out with Sir Jeremy in the morning, meeting the tenant farmers and seeing new beauties of the estate that had been too distant for her former pedestrian ramblings or too difficult to reach during their drive in the curricle.

She was happier than she had ever been in her life. Even in their prosperous days in Paris there had always been the chance that her father would lose that night and the next day would find them selling everything and moving into cheaper accommodations. At last she had security, something she hadn't known since her childhood, and this alone would have sufficed to make her cup of happiness overflow even without the affection of the servants, which was so generously given her. The only thing to spoil her total satisfaction was the irritating voice of her conscience. The more she found she had in common with Sir Jeremy, the more she felt she was cheating him. Every day drew her deeper into the web of her own making, every day she realized it would be more difficult to admit the truth.

Fortunately, there was enough to occupy Alfie's mind that she was able to put less amiable thoughts aside. There was a great deal of preparation to be done for the Chandlers' visit, and Alfie involved herself in every stage of it, from designating bedrooms to cutting and arranging flowers and helping the cook make delicate little pastries and candies. It was with some surprise that Alfie realized Sir Jeremy was looking forward to this event with the excitement of a small boy, since it would be the first time he had properly entertained at Stafford Hall in years. In addition to working out the basic comforts for his family, he was full of ideas for decorating the house and was nearly driving the poor gardener mad with his demands for more and more flowers.

Arthur Huxtable was underfoot a great deal of the time—when he was not underfoot at the Jennings household, where similar but much more lavish preparations were under way. He and Alfie were soon on familiar terms, and Arthur often sought her out when he was feeling particularly unwanted or useless. Today, he found her in the kitchen preparing some unknown but delectable-looking delicacy.

Alfie slapped his hands as he reached out for one, sending up a small puff of flour with the action. "You've had three already," she said severely. "Cook told me you were sneaking around here before."

"You needn't strike me," he said, a bit hurt.

Alfie grinned. "You needn't steal food. Goodness, don't they feed you enough at the Jennings'?"

Arthur looked offended at this remark, but instead of leaving, he sat down closer to the plate of delicacies, awaiting his chance. Alfie, however, kept a wary eye on him.

"What do you call these?" he finally ventured.

"Rat poison," Alfie said without hesitation. "We spread them out in the stable—they must look pretty because the rats are extremely clever and won't take anything that even resembles poison."

"Oh, come, I've had three already and I'm not dead yet."

"So you admit it! Well, don't worry, it's the fourth one that's fatal to human beings. Aren't you glad I stopped you?"

Arthur gave a wistful little sigh and started biting one of his fingernails.

Alfie looked at him sympathetically. "What's wrong—feeling left out?

"Curse it, Alfie," he said with sudden force, "it seems a chap has no more to say in his own wedding than the second footman—less, in fact, I saw them consulting *him* the other day."

Alfie chuckled. "Don't take it so badly. It's after the wedding that you have your say."

Arthur merely sighed again, feeling very persecuted. "I dunno, Alfie. Are all women like that? It used to be

Mary Ellen and I could sit for hours, just watching the clouds and holding hands. Now all she does is talk about the wedding and send me on errands, half of them made up, I'm sure, just to get me out of the way."

Alfie was trying hard to be understanding, but Arthur looked so ridiculous sitting there with that pitiful look on his face. "Cheer up," she said, "it only happens once. You just keep on doing all the errands and you'll be surprised when you hear Mary Ellen telling everyone what a help you've been. If you start getting in her way and giving your own orders, you'll be considered a nuisance."

"But it's not fair, I tell you," Arthur said. "Why, I have to run up to London tomorrow just to find some ribbon that's a certain shade of pink—none of the local pinks will do. Alfie, what am I doing running into women's shops?"

"Here, have a cake," Alfie said, holding one out.

Arthur took it absently. "That's an idea. I'll end it all right now by taking poison—give me a few more, just to be sure."

Alfie laughed. "Go on, now. Why don't you go out for a long walk or go bathing in the pond. That should clear your head."

Arthur stood up. "Yes, I'll drown m'self. I hear that's an easy way to go."

"Don't worry, Hux," Alfie said as he walked toward the door, stealing a few more cakes on the way, "you just have the pre-wedding doldrums. In less than a week it will all be over with."

"That's all very well, but will I last that long?" Arthur asked and he popped a cake into his mouth and left.

In a few more days everything was ready at Stafford Hall for the arrival of guests. Alfie was awaiting the

Chandlers with some misgivings, for she was afraid that Geoffrey would still be enamored of her, and she wasn't sure she could hold him at arm's length much longer. She realized with amusement that Lady Chandler was on her side, for her own reasons. How much more opposed Lady Chandler would be to a match between her son and Alfie if she knew who Alfie really was. The more Alfie considered it, though, the more she thought it likely that Geoffrey had formed a new attachment. He was at a fickle age, and they had not parted on very sociable terms. In fact, Alfie's behavior toward him had been that of an older sister toward a younger, slightly irritating brother.

Unfortunately, Alfie underestimated herself. She was looking very lovely on the day of the Chandler's arrival, in a dress of green, which was her best color, and her complexion was enhanced by a flush of excitement at playing hostess. She and Sir Jeremy greeted the Chandlers in the great hall, giving instructions left and right for bags to be taken up, fires lit if necessary, and tea served. It was quite a bustle indeed, for in addition to the six members of the Chandler family itself, there were also Lord Chandler's valet, Lady Chandler's maid, a governess for the two younger boys (who were quite put out by the thought that they needed a governess at all), and about five members of the Stafford Hall staff running about and getting organized.

Alfie gave a great sigh of relief when the last of them had been provided for and shipped up the stairs. She was happy, delightfully happy. Not even the thought that she was still deceiving all these people dampened her spirits at that moment, because she felt that the respect of the servants, the affections of the Chandlers, were for her,

Alfie, and not merely for Sir Jeremy's daughter.

She was startled out of her ecstatic reverie by the sound of her name being whispered from the stairway. Her heart sank as she recognized the voice and she turned around quickly. "Geoffrey! What's the matter with you?" she said, a bit annoyed.

He gave a stealthy glance around and Alfie was struck by how childish he looked, like a little boy who didn't want to be caught out doing something naughty.

"I say, Alfie," he said in a normal tone, after making certain no one was nearby, "I just had to see you alone for a minute. I missed you so." He came forward and before Alfie knew what was happening, his hands were on her shoulders.

"Geoffrey, really—"

"Alfie, don't say it's wrong. When I saw you at the door welcoming us all in, you looked like an angel at the gates of heaven."

Alfie laughed slightly and succeeded in wriggling out of his grasp. Geoffrey was hurt by her laughter and looked just like a puppy dog whose usually kind mistress had just slapped him.

"Don't be unkind, Alfie. Darling." He tested the word to see how it sounded and how she would take it.

"Geoffrey," she said sharply, "I am not your darling. Now please stop being so silly and go upstairs like a good boy."

But Geoffrey was not so easily put off. "You're so beautiful when you're angry, Alfie. Tell me—didn't you miss me just a little?"

Alfie sighed. "I can't really say that I gave it much thought."

"I've been thinking about you. I've never met anyone

like you before." To her dismay, he approached her again and she backed up, right against the wall.

"Geoffrey," she said firmly, "I have things to do. I have no desire to stand here listening to you recite worn-out phrases."

"Alfie, you must feel it, too," Geoffrey said.

"The only thing I feel right now is annoyed." She was beginning to get angry with herself for not being in better control of the situation as well as with Geoffrey for causing it. He approached her again, replacing his hands on her shoulders. "*Please*, Geoffrey."

"Please, Alfie, I must tell you something. Perhaps you'll feel different when I tell you."

With a sudden effort Alfie freed herself once again. "I don't want you to tell me anything, Geoffrey. You'll only regret it later. Let me just say that I am fond of you, but I think of you as a brother and I don't believe that feeling will ever change."

"It must, Alfie, I know it must. Don't you feel it? It's destiny."

"Geoffrey, it is *not* destiny. It is not anything. Now I think you had better go upstairs and change your clothes. We'll be dining shortly." With these words, she turned away from him sharply and walked into the study—simply because it was the closest room that had a door she could slam.

As she did this, making an admirable bang, she saw Sir Jeremy sitting at his desk, trying to control his laughter. "Well, if it isn't the angel from the gates of heaven," he said, a bit unsteadily.

"Don't tell me you heard all that?" she asked him with some consternation.

He nodded, not trusting himself to speak again.

"Well," Alfie said, sitting down, "you might at least have made some noises so he'd know you were here, instead of leaving me to fight him off all alone."

Sir Jeremy's laughter had died down and he was able to speak once more. "I was enjoying myself too much to do that. It's obvious my nephew has been reading too many novels. On the other hand, he might have a promising career in the theater if my sister would allow him to pursue it. She might, you know. I'm sure the talent comes from her."

Alfie's anger had faded rapidly and she joined Sir Jeremy in his laughter. "He really is difficult to take seriously," she agreed. "I had hoped his ardor would have cooled by now—we did almost nothing but argue the entire time I was in London."

"That has most likely increased your attraction for him," Sir Jeremy said wisely. "He thinks of you as a passionate woman, just as he thinks of himself as a passionate man."

Alfie giggled. "If you call that passion, I'd be afraid of the real thing."

"Yes," said Sir Jeremy, suddenly serious. He started rubbing a small spot on his desk, thinking deeply.

After a minute or so, Alfie stood up and said with forced cheerfulness, "I must change for dinner." Sir Jeremy looked up and their eyes met almost reluctantly. Alfie found it more difficult to tear herself away from Sir Jeremy's gaze than it had been to wriggle out of Geoffrey's grasp. Finally she gave him a tremulous smile and turned away quickly, running to her room as soon as she left the library.

That evening's dinner was but a prelude to the festivities that would begin the day after next at the wedding.

Everyone seemed to be in a holiday spirit, except for Geoffrey, who was brooding, doubtless fancying himself a star-crossed lover. Alfie was seated between George and Jason Chandler, who were feeling very festive indeed at being allowed to sit with the adults. The privilege *almost* made them forget the governess who had been forced upon them, but not quite since that notable personage was also present, spending most of her time frowning at Jason whenever that unfortunate boy chanced to do something, or even appeared as if he were thinking of doing something, untoward. Alfie kept them amused, though, and they very soon were feeling the brotherly affection toward her that she wished Geoffrey would adopt.

The conversation was monopolized by Lady Chandler and her eldest son, John. Alfie had seen little of John during her stay in London, and she hoped she would see even less of him now, for he was an obnoxious and overbearing boor. He was obviously his mother's darling, though, and she encouraged him to speak of his interests and accomplishments to the supreme boredom of the rest of the party. Evidently, he had been recently crossed in love, and Lady Chandler was doing her best to help him forget the pain of the incident. Alfie noticed Sir Jeremy exchanging sympathetic glances with Lord Chandler, and occasionally one fell in her direction, which she answered with a rueful grin.

Later that evening, Sir Jeremy sat alone in his study. The rest of the house had gone to bed early, tired out from the journey, but Sir Jeremy was not feeling especially tired and retreated to his study to do some reading. He was unable to keep his mind on the book, however; instead he was thinking of Alfie. He had to keep reminding himself that she was his daughter, for he found it difficult to remember otherwise. She's so damned attractive, he thought to himself, throwing the book down on his desk. He stood up and started pacing the room. What's wrong with me? he wondered. She's my daughter, my *daughter*. Then why am I reacting in this silly manner? It isn't natural that my heart should start beating faster when she looks at me in that certain way.

Damn it all, he thought, it's mostly her fault. She doesn't act like a proper daughter. She argues with me and tells me what to do. She doesn't sit quietly with her needlework as a daughter ought to, she comes in here and tells me why she thinks Dr. Johnson was a bag of wind and *Rasselas* a silly book. He doubted he knew any other woman who had even heard of Dr. Johnson. He kicked his desk fiercely.

Just then a knock came on the door. "Come in," Sir Jeremy snapped.

It was Arthur Huxtable. "Sorry, Jer, I didn't mean to disturb you. I was just coming in and heard some noise, thought you might want some company."

"I do." Sir Jeremy stopped his pacing. "Sit down, Hux." Arthur sat down obediently. "Tell me, Hux, do I seem normal to you?"

"Normal?" Arthur, feeling a bit sleepy after his full dinner and his ride back from the Jennings', was totally unprepared for this line of questioning.

"Yes, Hux, normal. Have I ever seemed odd to you?"

"Odd?" Poor Arthur had no idea what was expected of him. "What's wrong, Jer?"

"I don't know," Sir Jeremy said, sitting down. "I wish I did. It's all her fault." This last was muttered under his breath, but Arthur caught the drift of it and felt as if it explained everything.

"Oh, it's a woman, is it?" he said, suddenly wise. "Don't you know by now that you're never normal where a woman is concerned? Why, look at me—two months ago I was happy, free, not a care in the world. And now—"

Sir Jeremy smiled slightly. "I know, Hux, you're right. Of course a man can't be expected to behave rationally where a woman is concerned, but Hux—my own daughter?"

Arthur was again confused. "Eh?" he said lucidly.

"It's Alfie, Hux. I feel, well, more than fatherly toward her."

Arthur thought about this for a minute. Finally he said, "Jeremy, you've asked my opinion and I'll give it. There's nothing wrong with you. Alfie's a damned attractive woman, and smart, too. You haven't had time to learn how to be a father and she don't act much like a daughter. She seems almost too old to be your daughter, you know, for all she's only seventeen. Why, she's been giving *me* advice." He said this last with the air of one who had never required advice, but always dispensed it, as he was doing now. "Just you wait until next spring," he continued, "when there are eighteen men offering for her. You'll feel more fatherly then."

"Thanks, Hux, I suppose you're right. As you say, I've never been a father before, perhaps I am acting normally. I wish I knew another father to consult with. It's no good asking Richard, all he has are sons."

"Don't worry about it, Jer. For instance, if I hadn't met Mary Ellen first, and if Alfie weren't half a foot taller than me, I might be feeling a bit the same way, too."

They bade each other good night and went off to their rooms, but in spite of his friend's words, Sir Jeremy was still uneasy about his feelings toward Alfie. One remark of Arthur's struck him, though. "She seems almost too old to be your daughter." Damn her, she did. She was always coming up with some unexpectedly wise or educated remark, but Sir Jeremy had attributed that to her upbringing. Even with Geoffrey, though—she was three years younger than his nephew and had handled him as if she were an elder sister. On the other hand, she fit in so well at Stafford Hall and they had so many interests in common that it seemed almost impossible that that should be merely coincidence and not heredity. The whole thing was a puzzle, and although as a rule Sir Jeremy liked puzzles, he wasn't too fond of this one.

11

THE day of the wedding dawned bright and clear. Warmed by a beam of sunlight that had found its way between the drawn curtains, Alfie opened her eyes lazily. She didn't feel like getting up just yet, preferring to lie in her bed trying to remember a dream that she knew had been pleasant, although the details of it had escaped with her sleep.

She stretched her arms and legs deliciously, still reluctant to shake off the remnants of sleep—or perhaps more reluctant to go downstairs and start fighting Geoffrey off again, she thought with a private smile. He had been a nuisance all the day before, following her around like a stray dog. She almost laughed again when she thought of how she had tired him out riding—why, he had become almost manageable after that. It was almost fortunate that he fancied himself a nonpareil and had chosen one of Sir Jeremy's friskiest horses to accompany Alfie on her daily ride. The horse had been too much for him; he was used to a nice, dignified trot in a London park on a city horse that shied at nothing. He had stayed away from his father's estate too long and wasn't used to a long gallop across the country fields—he had even forgotten that one had to watch out for rabbit holes. Fortunately, neither he nor the horse had been physically injured, but Geoffrey's pride had suffered a severe blow, especially when Alfie could only look on and laugh as he lifted himself from the puddle and tried to scrape the mud off the elegant off-white pantaloons he had been so proud of earlier. He had been out of temper with her for the rest of the day, a state of affairs that was much easier for Alfie to endure than for Geoffrey to maintain. In fact, Alfie welcomed his sullen silence, and hoped that he, too, would realize they were unsuited.

She didn't expect his sulkiness to last until today, though, especially since Geoffrey had announced to her that she was forgiven just before they retired the night before. Alfie had been slightly annoyed when he informed her of this fact.

"You're forgiving me for putting a rabbit hole in your way?" she had asked.

Geoffrey had merely looked at her piteously. "You may pretend all you like, Alfie," he replied, "but you can't deny that Fate is throwing us together. She's on my side, Alfie."

"I'm sorry," Alfie said coldly, "but I have never been properly introduced to this person Fate, and I dislike taking the advice of strangers." With that she had left Geoffrey gaping moonishly after her.

Alfie thought about the conversation now as she lay in her bed, still basking in the morning sunlight trickling in between the curtains. Poor Geoffrey, she thought, she was being so unkind to him—yet, it was so hard not to be. And it seemed the more unpleasant she was, the more he adored her and fawned on her. Perhaps she should change her tactics—if she were a little more agreeable, he might lose interest. But she was hesitant to pursue such a course of action for fear it might work the opposite effect and cause Geoffrey to think she was finally succumbing to his attentions and that he should increase them accordingly. No, she would simply have to be firm with him and ask him plainly to leave her alone.

Later on, as Hawkins helped her dress, Alfie suddenly realized that this had been the first time she had awakened at Stafford Hall without the fear of disclosure foremost in her mind. So I have *something* to thank Geoffrey for, she thought, although I can't tell him so. Perhaps I will be a little more charitable toward him today. After all, the Chandlers will be leaving tomorrow and then I'll be free of him at least until Christmas.

With that noble resolution she went happily down to the breakfast room, where she found the object of her recent thoughts moodily poking at a heap of food. Alfie could have laughed at the perfect picture of unrequited love he presented, but she swallowed her laughter valiantly and greeted him as if they were on the best of terms.

"Good morning, Geoffrey," she said cheerfully.

Geoffrey looked up glumly. "I suppose it must be," he admitted, somewhat reluctantly.

Alfie realized it was going to be more difficult than she had supposed. "Come, Geoffrey, you don't have a proper wedding spirit."

Geoffrey gave a grunt, fraught with sarcasm. "You're a fine one to speak of wedding spirit," he said, addressing the tablecloth.

"Now, don't be bitter," Alfie said.

Geoffrey gave a heartrending sigh in reply.

Alfie tried to ignore his theatrics. "Am I late or was everyone else early this morning?" she asked, now with a forced brightness, as she noticed that the food laid out on the sideboard was cold and nearly depleted.

"Both, most likely," Geoffrey replied. "My uncle has taken George and Jason out to look at the horses again."

Alfie decided she was making progress, as this was the most civil thing he had yet said. She took up a plate and supplied herself with some breakfast, not because she was particularly hungry, but just for something to do as she worked out what she should say to her adopted cousin. She sat down at the table with her plate.

"Geoffrey," she said at long last, after running out of ways to arrange her napkin on her lap, "I wish you'd stop being so silly. Let's call a truce."

"A truce? I wasn't aware we were at war." Geoffrey was aloof.

"Come now, you know what I mean. You stop making advances and I'll stop being unkind. We can be friends." Alfie waited for his answer, trying to see the expression in his downcast eyes. Finally she gave up. "Well, don't say I didn't try," and she stood up to leave the room, her food untouched.

"Alfie." Geoffrey's voice was very low, but Alfie sat down again. He smiled. "I'm sorry, Alfie, we'll have a truce." He held out his hand to her and Alfie solemnly shook it, while Geoffrey just as solemnly informed her that she was a brick. Alfie had her first opportunity to keep the truce by not saying that she disliked being called a piece of building material.

The wedding was quite a lovely affair, taking place in a half-ruined little chapel where the curling vines and open roof provided a pleasant pastoral setting, although this atmosphere was broken now and then by a giggle from an irrepressible Miss Jennings. All four of the younger girls were dressed in various shades of pink— Alfie wondered which was the one Arthur had gone to London to find—and had shining pink faces to match. But by the end of the ceremony, Mrs. Jennings was ready to lock all of them in the nursery, except for the fact that she was unable to detect the exact source of the noise, and she always attempted to be fair in her administration of discipline—a fact the girls often took advantage of. Instead, Mrs. Jennings took more and more frequent sniffs from a small bottle she always had handy and put on one of her most martyred expressions, in the hopes that guilt alone would induce her children to behave.

However, the nuptial knot was tied without a hitch and no one seemed happier than Arthur Huxtable himself. Colonel Jennings' joy was marred only by the knowledge that he had four more daughters left—he looked upon Mary Ellen's wedding as merely the first victory in a long war. Indeed, he led the procession of carriages back to the house mounted on a large-boned stallion, looking much as if he were leading the troops home from successful battle.

The day was quite warm, but all sorts of cooling drinks had been provided and awnings had been set up on the lawns to give some shaded spots where there were few trees. The ballroom had been decorated lavishly with flowers, and all the doors and windows stood open to relieve the heat. Mrs. Arthur Huxtable was bustling about, properly blushing under her freckles and indeed managing to do everything properly. Sir Jeremy realized very quickly that Arthur had made a perfect choice; for all her blushes and maidenly reserve, it was obvious that Mary Ellen was the only one present who had any control over the operations of the wedding breakfast. Sir Jeremy watched her with admiration as she successfully took care of three servants, Arthur, Arthur's mother, and her own mother almost all at the same time.

"I'll never understand why they call it a wedding breakfast when it takes place in the middle of the afternoon," he heard a voice remark in his ear.

Sir Jeremy turned from his observation of the bride and smiled at Alfie, who was standing beside him, a glass of champagne in her hand. "Tradition, I suppose," he replied. "Just like everything else about a wedding."

"Well, it certainly seems a nice tradition," Alfie said. "What were you watching? You seemed miles away."

"I was admiring the bride. I am told it is the thing to do at a wedding."

Alfie laughed lightly. "Another tradition," she said as she turned her gaze toward Mary Ellen. "She does seem nice, though, and she certainly has a great deal of presence for her age."

Sir Jeremy looked at her quizzically. "That sounds odd coming from someone who can't be any older than she is."

Alfie felt her heart thump as she realized the mistake she had nearly made, but she was able to reply, "Oh, but I think of myself as infinitely older, having looked after my stepfather as I had to."

Sir Jeremy did not reply, but his searching glance made

Alfie extremely uncomfortable. "And where is your constant admirer?" he finally asked.

Alfie laughed, glad of the chance to change the subject. "I hope he's met someone else. The next Miss Jennings is fifteen and seems to be as self-contained as her elder sister."

"Perhaps more," Sir Jeremy said. "Mary Ellen was quite tongue-tied the first time I met her."

"Ah, but you would frighten the—" Alfie suddenly stopped, her face paling noticeably as her eyes seemed to be fixed on some distant point in the room.

"Are you feeling well?" Sir Jeremy asked with some concern.

"Yes—no. In fact, I think I'm feeling a bit faint. It must be the heat." She turned away quickly and left Sir Jeremy standing alone. He looked in the direction she seemed to have been looking in, but could not discover any cause for her peculiar behavior. He was about to go after her, when some old acquaintance suddenly came up to him and claimed his attention. He had never really liked the fellow and would have gladly strangled him at that moment.

Alfie really did think she was going to be ill as she rushed into an empty room to collect her thoughts. Had he seen her, she wondered. He must have, she was sure he had met her eyes. She felt very faint indeed as she thought about that sickening moment again.

How could this have happened? In all her time in Paris she had known but one Englishman—for him to suddenly turn up in the most unexpected place was indeed a stroke of bad luck. She sat down weakly in the closest chair. One moment she had been enjoying herself, chatting with Sir Jeremy, the next moment she had seen Damon

Whitfield, a man she had hated for eight years, a man who had given her nightmares for a year after she had first met him. It had taken her so long to exorcise him from her memory; had he returned only to torment her again?

Suddenly a new and worse fear made itself known to Alfie's troubled mind. At first it had been merely his presence that had caused her to react so violently, but suddenly she was desperately afraid that he would speak to Sir Jeremy—or anyone—and reveal her true identity. A chance word, an accidental phrase in the wrong ear, and her secret would be known and doubtless repeated in the most unflattering manner.

Alfie suddenly noticed that in her anguish she had nearly destroyed one of the lace flowers adorning her dress. She stood up again, locking her hands behind her back, pacing the room restlessly. What should she do? Should she tell Sir Jeremy the truth, immediately, before he had a chance to hear it from unkind lips? She stopped short and sat down again as a new thought struck her. Whitfield was too wily to let the truth just slip out—not when he could use it to his own advantage. Alfie had heard many tales of his nefarious dealings; the very reason he had had to leave Paris was that one of his blackmail schemes had misfired.

This new thought revived her somewhat, for Alfie would prefer even blackmail to Sir Jeremy's learning her secret, especially from Damon Whitfield, but it was very small comfort indeed for it turned her fears in a new direction. Would he attempt to renew the advances that had been stopped so abruptly seven years ago? She shuddered at the very thought of his coming near her, with his gross bulk and that unspeakable look in his eyes that had haunted her for months long ago—but that might well be the price he would require.

She was suddenly interrupted in her mental torture by the sound of a step in the doorway. She looked up, almost expecting to see Whitfield himself standing before her. It was only Lord Chandler, though, looking very kind and concerned.

"Are you quite all right?" he asked. "Jeremy told me you had suddenly been taken ill. He would have come himself, but he seems to have been nabbed by some old school chum. Is there anything I can do? Fetch you a glass of something, perhaps?"

Alfie smiled at him weakly, but gratefully. "No, thank you. I think I'll be all right now. It was just a touch of heat."

He came over and sat next to her. "Yes, it is a bit warm out there, but this has come on very suddenly. I hope"— he looked a trifle embarrassed—"I hope my son hasn't been bothering you too much. I would speak to him, but I'm sure that would only encourage him."

Alfie smiled again. "No, Geoffrey and I have declared a truce, as we call it. And I'm certain you're right about speaking to him—he really is most perverse."

"I'm afraid he takes after his mother," Lord Chandler said. "She always was a contrary one. Tell her one thing and she'll go out and do just the opposite, so you must learn to tell her not to do the thing you want her to do. Sounds complicated, I know, but it works quite well once you've had some practice. Only way I've found that does work."

Alfie laughed. She was beginning to feel much better now. Lord Chandler seemed to have a knack for getting one's mind off one's problems. She began to think about her situation in a calmer manner. Perhaps she would never see Damon Whitfield again. Certainly she must be more careful in the future, but today was surely an accident. He probably hadn't seen her, and if he had, he most likely hadn't recognized her. After all, it had been more than seven years since he had last set eyes on her, and here she was dressed as a seventeen-year-old again. Perhaps he might have noticed a likeness, but how could he connect the daughter of Sir Jeremy Stafford, Baronet, with the daughter of Robert Marsh, gambler?

She smiled again at Lord Chandler, who seemed to be waiting for her to completely recover from her "touch of heat."

"That's better," he said. "Come now, this is a wedding. You must enjoy yourself and feel festive."

"Thank you," she said. "I—I'll just take a look around the room first, to see if it's cooled down at all."

Lord Chandler looked at her with sudden wisdom. "Tell me who it is you fear and I'll see if he has left."

Alfie was embarrassed that the cause of her distress was so obvious. She wondered if Sir Jeremy, too, had realized what alarmed her. Well, it's too late now, she thought.

"It was just someone I thought I might have met in Paris. Someone unpleasant," she said hesitantly. "Most likely it isn't the same person at all."

"Ah, well, what did he look like?"

"A large man, puffy face. He's wearing a rather bright waistcoat. Yellow, I think."

"Ah, that would be Damon Whitfield," Lord Chandler said. "I agree he's enough to make any decent girl feel faint—can't imagine how he came to be here today. He may be accepted in certain London circles, but our honest country folk won't have anything to do with him. But he can't be the same person you knew—Whitfield hasn't been in Paris in years. Plotting against the king, it was rumored." He said this last in a confidential tone, almost as if it weren't proper for him to repeat it to Alfie.

Alfie gave a brave but false smile. "Well, then, I have nothing to fear, have I?" Her legs still shaky, she followed Lord Chandler back into the reception hall.

12

LUCKILY, it seemed Damon Whitfield had gone by the time Alfie ventured forth from the small room, for she did not see him again. However, she was unable to rid herself of a feeling of uneasiness, a feeling that everywhere she turned she would see him again, staring at her, leering at her. She realized that it had been stupid of her to react so violently to his presence, for if he had indeed been watching her or even looking in her direction, her behavior undoubtedly had confirmed her identity. And though she tried to convince herself to the contrary, she knew that if they met face to face, he couldn't fail to recognize her as the Alfreda Marsh he had known. She might be introduced to him as Miss Stafford, but a name alone could not change her face nor validate the story of her miraculous reappearance from the dead that would accompany such an introduction. Alfie passed the rest of the afternoon in a daze, trying to smile and chat as she was introduced to many of the neighbors in the county, but all the time she suffered a gnawing fear that Whitfield would return and a dread of the price she would have to pay for his silence.

These new fears were added to those she had been harboring since the beginning of her masquerade, and she was unable to hide the effects of the sleeplessness they caused her, although she attempted to go through her normal daily routines. The day after the wedding was another fine warm day, and after seeing the Chandlers off on their journey back to London, Alfie took the opportunity to go out to the garden and cut some of the summer flowers that were at the peak of their bloom. She hoped that the fresh air would revive her and that some useful occupation would take her mind off herself, but her task was not having its desired effect. Instead, each flower had assumed the hideous features of Damon Whitfield, and with each snip of her garden shears, she felt she was inflicting a mortal wound upon him.

She was unaware that Sir Jeremy had come up behind her and was watching her movements with interest. She jumped when he finally spoke, inquiring if she was feeling quite well.

"Oh, quite well, thank you," Alfie said, but the look in her eyes belied her statement. "You startled me, sneaking up as you did." She tried to make her voice light, but failed miserably.

"Is something troubling you?" Sir Jeremy asked, concerned. "You seem to have it in for those flowers." Alfie did not respond but merely snipped listlessly at a few more blooms. "Come, if you can't confide in me, whom can you confide in?"

Alfie laughed nervously. "Why, no one, of course." She wished very much that she could confide in him, for the burden of her secret was becoming too heavy to bear alone. But she could not bear to hurt Sir Jeremy with the truth. She suddenly felt a bit dizzy and sat down quickly in the shade.

"I believe I *am* feeling a bit out of sorts," she said.

Sir Jeremy's brows creased. "You certainly haven't been yourself since yesterday. Perhaps you caught a chill at the wedding. I was worried when you had that dizzy spell. Often it's the combination of the hot weather and the cold drinks. You should have had tea instead of champagne."

"Yes," Alfie said, snatching at straws. "That must be it. I think I'll go and lie down now and perhaps I'll feel better." She laid down her gardening tools and basket of flowers and wiped her hands on the coarse smock that protected her dress. As she was untying the strings, Wilson came up to Sir Jeremy.

"Sir Jeremy, a Mr. Whitfield is here to see you," he announced.

Alfie felt as if every drop of blood had drained from her body. He *had* noticed her yesterday, her last hope was gone. Doubtless he had inquired about her and found out who she was pretending to be. Would he attempt to blackmail Sir Jeremy? But surely he couldn't believe he would have any success.

"Whitfield?" Sir Jeremy exclaimed. "What the devil does he want?"

"I'm sure I don't know, sir," Wilson replied, the disapproval in his voice indicating his opinion of this visitor.

"Well, show him into the library," Sir Jeremy said. He turned back to Alfie. "Indeed, you don't look at all well, Alfie. I suggest you go straight to bed."

Alfie was only too glad to take his suggestion.

Sir Jeremy was puzzled by his visitor. He barely knew Damon Whitfield, and what he knew of him he certainly didn't care for. Although Whitfield was recognized in London circles, he was a notorious gambler and womanizer, and Sir Jeremy had heard of his reputation as a blackmailer. He gave a peculiar smile at that thought. If Whitfield had come to blackmail him, he would find an unwilling customer. Sir Jeremy cared nothing for his reputation and he knew of nothing he had done that was blackmailable; but farfetched as the idea seemed, he could think of no other reason for a call from Damon Whitfield.

Whitfield had already made himself comfortable in the library when Sir Jeremy entered. He stood halfway up to greet Sir Jeremy, but immediately sat down again, awaiting no invitation. Damned impudence, Sir Jeremy thought, sitting on the edge of his desk, but he said, "And to what do I owe the honor of this visit?"

Whitfield's thick lips formed a close approximation of a smile—as close as they would ever come to the real thing. "Sir Jeremy," he said, his voice smooth and damnably condescending, "is it unusual for one of the landed gentry to pay a visit on his neighbor?"

Sir Jeremy raised an eyebrow. "And since when have you been one of the landed gentry, Whitfield?"

Whitfield made a series of grunting noises that were supposed to pass for laughter. "Since a very lucky card game several weeks ago, I have been entitled to consider myself as such."

Sir Jeremy snorted. "I might have guessed."

Whitfield chose to ignore Sir Jeremy's implication and continued. "Lovely wedding, that of your friend Huxtable, despite the rather diminutive stature of the bridal couple. They seemed—"

"Come to the point, Whitfield," Sir Jeremy interrupted, losing patience. "I'm sure you didn't come here for a social chat."

"My dear Sir Jeremy, I *am* coming to the point. That lovely scene of marital joy awakened tender feelings in my own bosom."

Sir Jeremy snorted again.

"Now, now, Sir Jeremy. There is no reason for you to imply that I have no tender feelings." He licked his lips. "Fortunately, my tender feelings immediately found an outlet—in your lovely daughter, Sir Jeremy."

Sir Jeremy stood up, barely keeping hold of his temper.

Whitfield's sneer broadened. "Now, Sir Jeremy, let us not lose our tempers. I believe I am doing the proper thing by coming to you first. I wish to—what is that pleasant little phrase? I wish to pay court to your daughter." He gave a strange emphasis to the word daughter.

Sir Jeremy's eyes narrowed. "Over my dead body, Whitfield."

"My, aren't we melodramatic," Whitfield said, his eyes narrowing in response. "Don't you think some of the decision lies with Alfreda—or do you intend to be a tyrannical father? You can't have had much practice at it from what I hear."

"Alfie would have the choice if she were allowed the opportunity of meeting you, which she will not have in this house, nor any other house if I have anything to say about it. If you ever win the affections of my daughter"— a twisted smile appeared on his face—"which I sincerely believe to be impossible, you will never do so under my auspices. Furthermore, even if Alfie wished to marry you, I would, as you say, become a tyrannical father and forbid it."

"Do I take it, then, that you are inviting me to conduct a surreptitious courtship of your daughter? What an amusing prospect."

"I am inviting you to do nothing but leave my house. We can have nothing of value or interest to say to each other—now or ever." Sir Jeremy rang for Wilson, with such force that he nearly pulled the rope down. "I am *asking* you to leave now, but if I ever see you on or near my estate again, I shall take stronger measures to ensure that you do not return. You may already know, Whitfield, that the ownership of land does not automatically make one a gentleman, entitled to court gentlemen's daughters. You would not be a gentleman if you won half the British Empire in a card game."

Wilson came to the door and Sir Jeremy indicated that he was to show Whitfield out. Whitfield saw that he was to have no choice in the matter, but as he was leaving, he turned back to Sir Jeremy, the viciousness he had been hiding during his visit obvious now. "You will live to regret those words, Sir Jeremy," he said, and left.

In spite of himself, Sir Jeremy almost laughed out loud at Whitfield's dramatic exit line, but he was still too furious to allow himself that pleasure. Besides that, Whitfield's entire purpose in coming to see him was a mystery to Sir Jeremy. Surely the man wasn't cocky enough to believe that any real gentleman would allow his daughter to marry that profligate. Hadn't Whitfield known his visit would be fruitless? Or had he some reason to suppose otherwise?

Once again Sir Jeremy's thoughts returned to Alfie.

Was this another piece of the puzzle she was? His feelings toward her were confusing and upsetting; he was not quite sure whether he had been so emphatic with Whitfield because he had felt like an overprotective father or like a jealous lover. He had always prided himself on his powers of observation, and there were certain things he had observed about Alfie that made him wonder if she was being entirely truthful with him when she said she was his daughter. One part of him did not wish to learn the truth, if there was a truth to be learned, because that would mean she had been lying to him all this time. He had suffered too much from his marriage and had no desire to be further hurt and angered by a disloyal woman. The other part of him, however, wished that he might discover that she was indeed not his daughter, for he felt no other way of reconciling himself to the attraction she held for him. This visit from Whitfield must have something to do with Alfie's former life, before she discovered she was—or decided to become—Alfreda Stafford. Sir Jeremy was not certain of anything, though, except that he would very shortly be taking a trip to London, a trip he had been putting off because he did not wish to admit to himself the necessity for it.

He sighed and rang again for Wilson, who appeared almost immediately.

"Wilson," Sir Jeremy said, "I shall be leaving for London early tomorrow morning. Please be sure everything is ready."

"Very good, sir," Wilson replied, exhibiting no surprise at the suddenness of this journey.

"Oh, and Wilson"—Sir Jeremy smiled crookedly—"if Damon Whitfield ever has the audacity to call again, or even to set foot on the estate, you have my full permission to take whatever measures you see fit to expel him. Give that message to the rest of the staff, too—I won't have him around here."

"My pleasure, Sir Jeremy," Wilson said, with a glint in his eyes that indicated it certainly would be his pleasure to forcibly evict Whitfield from Stafford, personally.

Meanwhile, Alfie was going through her own torments. She longed desperately to tell Sir Jeremy everything, but she couldn't bear to disappoint him so after all the time and money and affection he had lavished on her. She toyed with the idea of running off to a convent, and almost laughed at the extremity of such an action; but the idea of running away stayed in her mind. She would not make any definite decision now, she thought, but would wait and see what Damon Whitfield had come to see Sir Jeremy about. Nevertheless, she was beginning to see that such a departure was the only possible ending to her little charade. How could she possibly spend the rest of her life living a lie?

These thoughts were painful to her, and not for the first time she wished she had never begun the deception in the first place. No matter what she did it seemed she would be hurting Sir Jeremy, the person she wished most to please. If only there were someone she could talk to— but the only one she wished to talk to was Sir Jeremy. She longed simply to rest her head on his shoulder and cry her eyes out, begging his forgiveness, even though she didn't deserve it. She deserved nothing from him—and especially not his love.

How much easier it would have been had Sir Jeremy been an old man, as she had expected, she told herself for the thousandth time. It would have been so easy to

deceive him then, but he was young and handsome, and
worst of all, she realized ruefully, she had fallen in love
with him. The things she had built her youthful dreams
on had come true at last, but certainly not in the way she
had planned. Through her own scheming she had trapped
herself into a position from which there was no happy
escape. If only she had fallen in love with anyone but Sir
Jeremy. Even Arthur Huxtable would have been a more
convenient object of her affections—she could have loved
him silently from afar, perhaps become a kind of maiden
aunt to his children, and Arthur certainly wouldn't have
minded or even noticed. But there was no way she could
speak her love for Sir Jeremy without admitting at the
same time that she had been cheating him.

Alfie managed to collect herself by dinnertime. She
wasn't especially hungry, but she could wait no longer to
learn the purpose of Damon Whitfield's visit. She felt
very worn out as she went down to the drawing room, and
the dark circles under her eyes emphasized her emotional
and physical exhaustion.

Sir Jeremy was already seated there, apparently deep
in thought. He didn't hear Alfie come in and she stood
for a moment watching him, wondering again if she
should just tell him everything right now. He looked up
suddenly and smiled at her, his characteristic crooked
smile. Alfie lowered her eyes, afraid he might see in them
her newly discovered love for him.

Sir Jeremy arose. "So, my dear," he said, "it seems
that it will be very difficult for me to keep your charms
hidden, even if I wanted to. You have just received your
first proposal of marriage."

"What?" Alfie asked blankly.

"It seems that Damon Whitfield saw you at the wedding the other day. He has just been here to ask permission to pay you court."

"And what was your answer?" Alfie was apprehensive.

"I sent him packing, of course. Deuced impudence of the man."

Alfie was surprised by the sudden fire in his eyes. "Thank you," she said, smiling almost shyly. "I saw him at the wedding and thought him dreadful." She felt relieved that her secret was safe for a little while longer, but how much longer? She realized with a sudden flash of insight that Damon Whitfield would not unmask her, not while there was a chance he could marry her as Sir Jeremy's daughter and have both her and a settlement from Sir Jeremy's fortune—and even, if he lived long enough, Stafford itself. It was a clever game, she thought, but she would not play it with him.

Sir Jeremy held out his arm. "Come, my dear, let us go in and eat our dinner. I'm afraid you will be finding it rather dull here after tonight now that our company and our lodger have gone, and since I must leave for London early tomorrow morning." His heart gave a leap as he noticed the look of consternation in her eyes. Was she disappointed because he was leaving or was she afraid that he had discovered her secret, if indeed she had a secret? He wished that she would confide in him—he would do anything to hear the truth from her own lips so that he might keep faith in her. He couldn't bear the torment of uncertainty much longer. Damnit, why did he have to fall in love with such women?

Alfie barely touched her food during dinner, and found it difficult to make even the most trivial conversation. She pleaded a headache very early—which indeed she did have—and rose to leave the table, wishing Sir Jeremy a very hasty farewell.

13

.

$\mathcal{A}$ LFIE arose early the next morning, but it was not early enough to see Sir Jeremy off. She missed him already—though he had barely been gone an hour, she suddenly felt lonelier than she had since she first arrived in Stafford Hall. Not even Arthur Huxtable was there to amuse her, if she could possibly be amused in her present state of mind. She decided to go for her morning ride to dispel the cobwebs of despondence and hopelessness that were promising to become permanent companions.

But while she went through the motions of her usual routine, she was unable to hide the fact that she was not feeling her best. Even Hawkins remarked upon her behavior. "I declare, miss, you just haven't been yourself for the past few days. It's my belief you're sickening for something." Of course, if Alfie let Hawkins have her way, she'd be tucked into bed and tied up with red flannel, a steaming kettle in the corner. And Alfie knew that certainly wouldn't cure what she was sickening from.

The only thing she had to occupy her mind during the long, boring days of Sir Jeremy's absence was her plan of flight, for she had decided it was inevitable that she must leave. She could not hide her feelings or her identity from Sir Jeremy much longer, and could certainly not remain at Stafford once she had revealed herself. Part of her reasoning was plain cowardice, and Alfie admitted as much to herself. She was simply afraid of what Sir Jeremy might do or say—or most especially, what the expression on his face would be if she were to tell him the truth directly. Thus she would leave him a note explaining the matter, and need never look him in the eyes again.

As she thought back, she knew that she should have realized a deception as she had undertaken could only end in disclosure; she could not have continued it for the rest of her life. But she had been so sure of herself, so sure that she could handle the situation, she had not thought further ahead than how to convince Sir Jeremy she was his daughter in the first place. Of course, she couldn't have known that she would fall in love with him, but that was small consolation in the face of her present predicament.

Why had she been so stupid? She should be off teaching in some remote county, not passing herself off as the daughter of a baronet. Then she would be faced only with a life of boredom instead of the life of self-recrimination she now saw before her, for deceiving the only man she had ever loved.

So once again Alfie started planning a departure into a new life, although all the hopefulness that had accompanied her last departure was now gone. She knew she would need some money for passage, but all she had were a few gold trinkets she had purchased with Sir Jeremy's money in London. She was sure she would not get much for them, but they would have to do, and it was still more than she liked to take, for by rights she should be leaving with nothing more than she had arrived with. The only justification for taking anything at all was so she wouldn't starve to death.

Sir Jeremy had not said how long he would be in London. It could be weeks for all she knew, for neither had he stated what his business there was. Perhaps she would leave before he returned, but she hoped that she wouldn't have to do that, because she wished to see him once more in her life, if only to thank him in some way for all he had done for her. During his absence she made her morning ride a regular routine, for she found it was the only thing that even slightly took her mind off the desolate life ahead of her; she had even lost interest in reading for the moment, finding it difficult to keep her mind on any book when her own problems were so pressing.

Alfie was taking such a ride on the fourth morning after Sir Jeremy had left, trying to concentrate on holding herself properly on the horse, to develop the grace and style of a good rider, when she heard another horse somewhere off behind her. She pulled up to see who it could be—for one happy, wild moment she thought it might be Sir Jeremy—but as soon as she saw the rider, her heart froze. She couldn't fail to recognize that huge, hulking body in a crowd of thousands. She thought for an instant of immediately galloping off, but he was too close to her by now and would undoubtedly catch up with her.

She let her horse go on at a slow trot, resigning herself to the interview that must follow. Sure enough, Damon Whitfield rode up beside her and said, with excessive politeness, "Good morning, Miss Stafford."

His mocking emphasis on her name was obvious and she didn't reply but merely gave him what she hoped was a withering glance.

"Let us not be so standoffish, Miss Stafford," he said, using the name as a barb. He added, as if he had given it some thought, "I must remark you look as youthful as a girl of seventeen."

Alfie grew annoyed. "What do you want?" she snapped.

His eyes glinted. "You know what I want, Miss Stafford. I must say your charms have not changed along with your name. In fact, I might say that they have been enhanced, Stafford being a name that commands much more respect than Marsh, to say nothing of much more money."

"Why don't you leave me alone?" she asked, feeling the hopelessness of such a request even as she made it.

"Now, Miss Stafford, if I left you alone, I would also feel it my duty to see that you left Sir Jeremy alone—and that would necessitate—"

"Leave Sir Jeremy out of this!" Alfie cried, growing more angry every second.

"Oh, now, we wouldn't want to do that, would we?" Whitfield said.

"Sir," Alfie said, drawing herself up, "not only do I object to your tone of voice, but I object to everything about you. That is another thing that has not changed about me."

"Yes," he said slowly, enjoying her wrath, "you always were a little spitfire, weren't you?"

"I must request that this conversation be ended. It is disgusting to me and can be of no benefit to you." Alfie dug her heels into the side of the horse and began to ride away.

Damon Whitfield was not to be so easily cast off. He quickly caught up with her, and steered his horse in front of hers, so she was forced to stop. "My dear Miss Stafford," he said, once again emphasing the name, "this interview should have benefit to me. My benefit will be your lovely self, and a tidy settlement from Sir Jeremy's lovely fortune. Or would you prefer that I go straight to Sir Jeremy with a little tale of a young girl I once knew in Paris, a certain Miss Alfreda Marsh? Then neither of us would benefit, and that would be a pity."

It would be difficult enough for Alfie herself to tell Sir Jeremy about her true identity, but she couldn't bear the thought of the information coming from Damon Whitfield. He would undoubtedly twist the truth into something more sordid than she had ever intended, perhaps even making more of what had been a distasteful slight acquaintance between them in Paris. Sir Jeremy might be able to forgive her in his heart if he knew that all she had hoped for was security, but Whitfield would most likely represent her as out for all Sir Jeremy possessed— if only to take some sort of petty revenge on her. She would be painted as the worst sort of scheming blackguard to Sir Jeremy, and while she knew her action had not been noble or honest, once she had assumed her role, she had tried to play it honestly. But Sir Jeremy would never believe that if he heard the story from Whitfield;

worse, he might think they had been in it together from the beginning.

"What do I have to do so you will leave me alone?" Alfie asked with forced calmness.

"My dear Miss Stafford, I am afraid I will never leave you alone," Damon Whitfield said, sneering. "We are not bargaining for that, but for your good name and Sir Jeremy's money, or hadn't you noticed?"

Alfie's eyes narrowed. "You'll never touch a penny of Sir Jeremy's money."

"Ah, well, now that's too bad. But I was thinking mainly of you, my dear. After all, I have plenty of money —a few thousand pounds one way or the other makes no difference. But if you were to marry me as Alfreda Stafford, there would be a tidy settlement for you, which I could manage for you very nicely with my other investments." He gave her his rough imitation of a smile. "And I had it so neatly planned—we would run off together, you and I, the forces of true love just too strong to be stopped by a disagreeable father. We would run to France, perhaps, and after we were married, perhaps we would let your *father* know where we were, so he could send us lots of money and make us comfortable and happy. And after a while we would return to my charming estate nearby and your *father* would introduce me to all the gentry in the county who were so ill advised as to snub me at the wedding of your friend last week."

Alfie listened to him in disgust. "I'm afraid I have even less interest in Sir Jeremy's money than I have in you."

Whitfield bared his teeth. "I'm afraid I can't believe *that*. Why else are you here, pretending to be his daughter, if not for his money? Come now, you're your father's daughter, my dear—your real father, that is. I have a feeling you and I have a great deal more in common than you wish to admit."

Alfie wanted to retort that there were many things she valued more than money, but she realized it would be useless. Instead, she said, "Why me? Surely there are other *genuine* gentlemen's daughters who would marry you and give you the same advantages. Sir Jeremy may discover I am not his daughter at any time and you would gain nothing."

Whitfield laughed. "You still fail to see the point, my dear. I would gain *you*. I would have had you seven years ago if your stupid father hadn't listened to your whinings, and I don't intend to be thwarted again. I happen to be a man who likes to get what he wants, however long it may take. Of course, I am willing to marry you only as long as you bring me the advantages of the Stafford name. If Sir Jeremy were to discover who you really are, you are the only one who would lose by it, for I intend to have you one way or the other."

Alfie realized with a wince what the other way would be. Whitfield would use her for a while and then discard her, much the worse for wear she had no doubt.

"But why France?" she asked suddenly. "I thought you were barred from that country."

"My, my, and you pretend to have no interest in me. Fortunately, my reason for avoiding France has conveniently died—such a shame—and it is a pleasant place to visit and I happen to have some new business to conduct there in the near future. So you see, there is nothing to stop my little plan except you, my dear."

Alfie was silent, thinking quickly. An idea was forming in her head that perhaps she could beat Whitfield at his own game and gain free passage to France as well. She would have to be careful, very careful, but although Damon Whitfield was a master of blackmail, she did not have a very high opinion of his intelligence in general. For one thing, he was a bad judge of people, tending to divide them into two categories, the ones who exploited and the ones who were exploitable. Sir Jeremy he obviously placed in the latter category. Whitfield must think him very stupid indeed—Sir Jeremy would never give him tuppence for marrying Alfie, and as to introducing him to the gentry, Alfie nearly laughed at the thought. Whitfield obviously didn't realize what kind of man he was dealing with—or what kind of woman. If she were to agree to his plan, he would suspect no other motive than that she did not wish Sir Jeremy to know who she really was so she could get his money and keep her reputation intact. Money was a motive Damon Whitfield could understand, for despite his words, every shilling mattered to him and the prospect of thousands of pounds was not to be sneezed at. Alfie realized if she let him believe that she had no wish for a fortune, she would have no weapon left to fight him with.

She spoke very slowly and carefully. "Am I to understand that if I do not agree to your little plan, you will run off and tell Sir Jeremy my real name so that I will not get any of his money? And that if he finds out, you intend to carry me off anyway?"

Whitfield snorted with laughter. "Finally, you are catching on, my dear."

"Let us wait, then," she said. "I need time to make plans. Obviously it's better for both of us if he still thinks of me as his daughter, but perhaps I could get his approval and we would not have to wait for the money. As you probably know, he is in London now."

He frowned. "I doubt he would approve—our only course of action can be to marry first without his knowledge." He looked at her sharply. "And don't think you can convince him to make a settlement for me to leave you alone. As soon as you do that, I will tell him who you are and take you with me anyway—as I said. I do not like to be thwarted, especially by a scheming chit who might think she can get the better of me."

"Let us wait, nevertheless," Alfie said. "I need time to get ready."

Whitfield's tone was menacing. "I warn you, I will not wait long. I will meet you here again in a week's time, with my carriage. If you are not ready by then, I will go to Sir Jeremy."

"I understand," Alfie said, eager to end the conversation. "In a week's time. Now, please, leave me alone."

Whitfield grinned, displaying a set of tobacco-stained teeth. "And if you are thinking of slipping away, don't worry, I will find you again if it takes another seven years. And then I will not bargain with you, but you will come with me on my own terms."

Alfie's one thought at that moment was to get away as quickly as she could, and she barely heard the threat. She rode toward the house, upset by the interview and unsure whether she had done the right thing. One thing she had accomplished, though; there would be little chance of her seeing him again for a week, and she could work out her plans more carefully. She urged her horse into a gallop and felt much better for the exercise.

Her head clear again, she suddenly decided to stop moping around. Her decision had been made, she must leave. Her plans needed only to be made more definite and put into action. When Sir Jeremy returned—if he returned before she left—she didn't want to seem quite as despondent as she had been since the wedding. If she saw him a last time, she wanted at least to leave some pleasant memory with him.

14

$\mathcal{A}$ S the week drew on and Alfie's next meeting with
Whitfield drew nearer, Sir Jeremy still had not returned
and Alfie was beginning to believe she would never see
him again. She missed him more each day, and wondered
what kept him in town so long, yet part of her wished that
he wouldn't return before the week was up—a last meeting would only make her departure more painful. Besides
fearing that seeing him again might weaken her determina-
tion, she was apprehensive that if he arrived before or on
the day she was to meet Whitfield, her escape might be
discovered and a very nasty scene would result. She tried
to think of an alternate plan should that possibly arise,
but nothing she thought of seemed as safe as the one that
depended upon Sir Jeremy's continued absence. But while
her practical side knew it would be next to disastrous

should Sir Jeremy come back too soon, her heart longed to see him just once more.

She continued her rides each day, finding enjoyment and freedom in them—also realizing that where she was going she might not have the opportunity to do much riding. She supposed some of the better French schools might have stables and riding masters, but that certainly did not mean that the schoolmistresses would be allowed to make use of them. So Alfie counted off each day by how many morning rides were left to her, and by the time she reached her last but one, she thought her practical side would win, for it was the very next day that she was scheduled to run off with Damon Whitfield and Sir Jeremy had given no indication of returning. She smiled slyly to herself as she thought of what else was scheduled for tomorrow, if things went as planned.

Suddenly she heard hoofbeats nearby and her heart sank. Whitfield wasn't supposed to come until the next day—was he here already to badger her and make her life miserable? But as soon as she saw who the rider was, her pulse began to beat wildly.

"Sir Jeremy!" she called joyfully, all practical considerations forgotten in her delight at seeing him again. He spotted her and rode up to meet her.

"And have you been enjoying yourself while I was gone?" he asked as soon as he was close enough.

Alfie laughed. "Of course not. It's been deadly dull here without you."

"You are certainly looking much better than when I left."

"It was an instant transformation as soon as I saw you had returned."

Sir Jeremy's eyebrows puckered. "Then you will be

disappointed to hear that I am leaving again tomorrow."

Alfie's face showed the expected disappointment, but her practical side breathed a sigh of relief. "Why so soon?" she asked.

"I left some unfinished business in London," he replied. "I returned today only because I ran into the Huxtables and brought them down with me."

"They are back already? I thought they were to be gone a month."

Sir Jeremy smiled his crooked smile. "So did they, but it seems Mrs. Jennings has suffered another accident and requires the assistance of her eldest daughter."

Alfie frowned. "That seems a bit unfair to me," she said. "Poor Arthur, is his mother-in-law to be forever falling down and calling Mary Ellen to her side?"

"I believe it has something to do with four daughters running about the house, tripping her up. I hope it's a lesson to Arthur. Anyway, I've brought them here for dinner. There's no sense in their waiting upon Mrs. Jennings too soon."

Alfie brightened again at this news. "Oh, that's lovely. I was hoping to come to know Mary Ellen better, she seems so nice." Although it will be a short-lived acquaintance, she thought to herself.

Alfie was determined to make her last meal with Sir Jeremy a pleasant one, but it seemed that Sir Jeremy was preoccupied with his own thoughts. She kept a light conversation going at the dinner table, but while Arthur and Mary Ellen were being most amusing about their experiences in Belgium and Holland, Sir Jeremy was hardly listening. More than once Alfie directed some trifling remark toward him, only to find that he had no notion of what she was speaking. This necessarily dimmed Alfie's humor somewhat, as she wondered what was troubling him. However, their guests did not seem to notice Sir Jeremy's strange behavior, or politely pretended not to.

When Alfie and Mary Ellen retired to the drawing room, leaving Sir Jeremy and Arthur alone, Arthur proved that he had not been entirely blind to Sir Jeremy's behavior.

"All right, Jer, what's up?" he said bluntly, as soon as the ladies had withdrawn.

"Whatever do you mean, Hux?" Sir Jeremy asked.

"You know very well what I mean," Arthur said. "You've been sitting here in a brown study all during dinner and you expect me not to notice?"

Sir Jeremy smiled slightly. "You're too astute for me, Hux. How can I keep any secrets from you?"

"If you don't want to tell me, you needn't, you know," Arthur said, pouring himself some brandy. "I don't mean to pry, but I certainly can't help noticing that something is bothering you." He took a sip of the drink, watching Sir Jeremy carefully. "Is it Alfie still, Jeremy?"

"No, I certainly can't keep any secrets from you, Hux," Sir Jeremy said, his brows creasing. "Yes. I just don't know what to make of it, either."

"Make of what? She was behaving admirably tonight, while you—"

"Now, I don't need a lecture on proper dinner deportment, Hux." Sir Jeremy lowered his voice. "I've been to see an investigator at Scotland Yard."

Arthur's face went blank. "Whatever for?"

"To see if he can discover whether Alfie is indeed my daughter, or just pretending to be. Think of it, Hux. Any woman could have found those items and come here, saying she was my long-lost daughter. What way would I have of knowing for certain?"

"And you think Alfie might just be pretending to be your daughter?" Arthur asked. "But why ever would she do that? I mean, she's a nice, well-bred girl. Wouldn't she go to her own family instead of passing herself off as your offspring?"

"One would think so," Sir Jeremy said with a sarcastic note.

"Scotland Yard, eh?" Arthur said reflectively. "What are they like, Jer, these investigators?"

Sir Jeremy gave him an impatient glance. "They're just like ordinary constables, except they know how to find things out."

"And what have they found out so far?"

"Nothing." Sir Jeremy showed an obvious disappointment.

"And what do you want them to find out?" Arthur's tone was soft.

"I don't know, Hux." Sir Jeremy felt very old and very sad. "If she really is my daughter, then the way I feel toward her can't be normal. If she isn't my daughter, then the way I feel is perfectly normal, but it would mean that she is nothing more than another fortune-seeking woman, out for whatever she can get from me." His tone was bitter.

Arthur thought about this for a minute, and then said, "Knowing Alfie, that seems unlikely. She seems such an *honest* sort of person." He thought hard for a few moments, then exclaimed brightly, with the air of one who has discovered the ultimate solution, "Perhaps she isn't but truly believes she is."

"I don't know, Hux," Sir Jeremy said glumly, showing

none of Arthur's sudden optimism. "I've thought about that possibility, of course, but it seems that if she really believes it, she, too, would feel that our behavior toward each other has not always been exactly fatherly or daughterly. It seems she might have spoken to me about it.

"I don't know, Jer—p'rhaps she doesn't know how you feel, and wouldn't want to embarrass you, or herself, by laying all her cards out, as it were."

"Perhaps." Sir Jeremy smiled slightly. "That's what I want to believe. The only other alternative is to realize she's just out for my money. I'll know for certain soon, I hope. I'll be going back to London tomorrow to consult with them again. They sent me a message indicating that they had turned up some new information."

"It's too bad she isn't ugly," Arthur said in a philosophical tone.

Sir Jeremy smiled. "And how do you mean that?"

"Well, if she were ugly, you wouldn't have been attracted to her in the first place, and then you wouldn't have wondered if she were really your daughter and then—"

Sir Jeremy held up his hand in mock distress. "Enough! Your logic is inescapable, Hux. But enough of this, the subject is giving me a headache. Why don't you tell me about your voyages. I'm afraid I wasn't very attentive at dinner."

While the two men spoke over their cigars and brandy, Alfie and Mary Ellen were becoming better acquainted in the drawing room. Alfie soon found her first impression of Mary Ellen to be an accurate one. The younger woman was certainly not as educated or worldly as Alfie, and was actually quite shy around strangers, but she had an abundance of common sense that more than made up for any deficiencies in her character. Indeed, she had found this common sense extremely useful, in fact necessary, when she was growing up, for her mother was an ineffectual woman, incapable of running a large house and looking after five daughters, especially in India where she could barely communicate with the servants, let alone give them orders. Mary Ellen had, at a very early age, taken over a great many of her mother's responsibilities. Her only fear in getting married was that her mother would have no one to look after her, a fear she was in the process of disclosing to Alfie.

"I was almost certain she would find some excuse to call us back early," Mary Ellen was saying. "She's never been without me before, you know."

"Surely, your father must be able to look after her." Alfie did not say so, but she strongly and sincerely disapproved of Mrs. Jennings' behavior.

Mary Ellen giggled. "My father was wonderful when he had to command hundreds of men in India, but I'm afraid he just doesn't know what to make of my mother. And, of course, he has no idea how to handle English servants, either. He tends to bark at them as he used to at our Indian servants, and, of course, they resent being spoken to in broken English as if they didn't know their own language."

"I see," Alfie said. "It does seem rather unfair of your mother," she put forth mildly, not wishing to offend Mary Ellen but feeling it must be said.

Mary Ellen's eyebrows came together in childlike anguish. "Yes, I think so myself sometimes, but then I wonder if I'm just being selfish."

Alfie smiled kindly, realizing that Mary Ellen needed

some reassurance. "Don't be so noble," she said. "Your mother has four more daughters to look after her. You must concentrate on setting up your own household now."

Mary Ellen's wide brown eyes turned to Alfie trustingly. "I'm so glad to hear you say that. It's nice to hear it from an uninterested party, to know that I'm not just being beastly."

Alfie almost laughed at the thought of this little girl— for that is what she seemed—ever being beastly, but she could tell that Mary Ellen was truly concerned. Alfie felt very worldly and wise, giving advice to someone supposedly her own age, but Mary Ellen was begging for moral support and it was obviously Alfie's duty to provide it.

"Mary Ellen," she said finally, "it seems to me that if your mother continues to think you're available to run to her whenever she wishes it, she will tend to overuse the privilege. It may be difficult, but I think you must resist every now and then. Not enough to hurt her feelings, of course, but enough so she realizes you are not on this earth merely to cater to her every whim—or broken bone, as the case may be. She can begin to depend upon your next oldest sister for a change, and when *she* wants to leave the nest, you can repeat this bit of advice to her!"

Mary Ellen listened to this speech attentively, and when Alfie had finished, she suddenly jumped up and hugged her.

"Oh, thank you," she said. "You're so wise. It has always been such a trial for me to be the eldest, always dispensing advice and having nowhere to go to get some for myself." She backed away again, suddenly shy. "I would like it very much if you would allow me to think of you as a kind of older sister. Arthur's very understanding, of course, but there are some things he just can't help me with."

Alfie was very touched by Mary Ellen's confidence, and impulsively returned her hug. She knew how Mary Ellen felt with all her problems, for Alfie had no one to turn to either. She felt a twinge of remorse when she realized that they would never have the time to become close friends, as they desired, but she fought the thought, still not allowing anything to ruin her last evening at Stafford.

Her troubled mind set somewhat at ease, Mary Ellen began to describe her adventures abroad. Everything had been new and wonderful to her, and Alfie was grateful for her innocent chatter. She did not wish to think of what the next day would bring, and for the moment, with Mary Ellen's help, was successful in keeping her mind off the future.

Alfie was glad to see that Sir Jeremy appeared to be in a better frame of mind when he and Arthur joined them in the drawing room later on. Obviously, Arthur had been cheering him up, too. But the Huxtables did not remain much longer; since they were not spending the night at Stafford Hall, there was a ten-mile drive to make before they reached their beds. Alfie thought it almost too good to be true that she would thus have some time alone with Sir Jeremy.

When the Huxtables had left, Sir Jeremy suggested a game of chess, since the hour was still so early. In spite of his apparently improved spirits, Alfie found he still had something on his mind that prevented him from being very companionable. She thought of a thousand things to say in an effort to break the increasing silence, but could not begin a conversation with any of them as they all related to her imminent departure or her undaughterly regard for him. Sir Jeremy was similarly at a loss.

About the fifth move, Alfie finally tried to open the conversation. "I found Arthur's wife perfectly delightful," she said rather flatly.

"Yes," Sir Jeremy agreed, "lovely girl."

Alfie waited for him to continue, but he appeared to have said all that was on his mind. She gave a little shrug of her shoulders, a very French gesture indeed, and devoted her attention to the chess board.

The game did not last very long. Sir Jeremy was a brilliant player, and while Alfie was an apt student, she had only won one or two games from him before, but this evening she was able to beat him in very little time.

"You might have put up more of a struggle," she said with a smile.

"I apologize," Sir Jeremy said. "As you can probably tell, I have my mind on other things."

"That's certainly obvious—the business in London?" She wondered what this business could be, but for some reason was afraid to ask him directly.

"Yes, that's right." Sir Jeremy began to absently rearrange the chess pieces on the board.

"I certainly hope it's cleared up soon," Alfie said. "You don't seem to be of much use to anyone right now."

Sir Jeremy gave his crooked smile. "No, I suppose not," he said. "It should be concluded tomorrow when I return."

"Will you be leaving early?"

He looked at her quizzically. "I had intended to."

Alfie felt a bit uncomfortable at his tone, and she

thought suddenly that he must suspect her. How else to explain his strangely taciturn manner or his mysterious visit to London? She was glad she would be leaving the next day, she simply could not bear to be by when he learned the truth, for if he seemed so distant and unfamiliar with just a suspicion, what would he be like when he learned the whole truth? Alfie knew she would be shut out of his heart forever, but it would not be quite as hard for her to endure if she were not around to receive his recriminations directly.

Her voice was small when she spoke again. "I was wondering because—it's just that I haven't seen very much of you lately, except for this one evening." She smiled again suddenly. "You haven't had a chance to see how my riding has improved since we rode together only a short distance this morning. I've been practicing every day."

"I'm sorry," he said softly. "When I return, I'll ride out with you every morning."

"Yes," Alfie said, realizing that the opportunity would never arise. She couldn't bear it any longer—she felt she was about to cry. "I must go to bed now," she said abruptly, her voice tremulous and uncertain. She stood up, trying to keep her eyes downcast so Sir Jeremy would not be able to see the pain in them, but the temptation to take her last look at him was too great. Their eyes met, and, impulsively, Alfie ran over to him and kissed him on the cheek. She was gone in a moment, and her tears began to spill over before she reached the comfort of her bed.

15

SIR Jeremy Stafford climbed a few steps from the street and found himself at an impressive door marked "Police Headquarters, Scotland Yard." He squared his shoulders before opening the door; he disliked the musty scent that invariably greeted him in the narrow entrance hallway. He made his way to the door marked "Criminal Investigation Department." Since the department was barely a year old and as yet had but a small force of men assigned to it, the offices were tiny, and the waiting room had the appearance of a converted broom cupboard.

A thin inky clerk greeted him and invited him to be seated on one of the precarious-looking wooden chairs. Sir Jeremy indicated his preference for standing.

"I am here to see Inspector Hamm," he told the clerk. The clerk smiled politely and said, "Yes, I know, Sir

Jeremy," and he slunk away, presumably to inform his master of Sir Jeremy's arrival.

Sir Jeremy did not like the fact that his name was so well known here, though he might have expected it to be, for he had been there no less than three times in the previous two weeks and his impressive stature was not easily forgotten. His first visit had been to tell his tale and inquire if the police could discover anything. Inspector Hamm had seemed reluctant at first to take on such an investigation as Sir Jeremy required, since it was not exactly of a criminal nature, or at least not so seriously criminal as those the Yard was used to. But when Sir Jeremy expressed his disappointment with the department and his inclination to wonder at the value of it, comparing it unfavorably with the now extinct Bow Street Runners, the Inspector had indicated that the case might provide some useful experience for one of their junior men. Sir Jeremy's next two visits were to discover that Inspector Hamm and his investigators had discovered nothing, that is, nothing beyond what Sir Jeremy already knew—that Robert Marsh had raised a daughter in Paris. On his last visit, Mr. Hamm had suggested that further research might prove fruitless, but he had promised to do his best. Of course, Mr. Hamm's best was represented to Sir Jeremy as infinitely superior to anything a country constable could do, an indirect reply to a remark Sir Jeremy had made about preferring the country to London.

In a few minutes, Sir Jeremy was shown into the eminent Inspector Hamm's office. Mr. Hamm's fawning manner seemed inappropriate for one used to dealing with criminals of all types, but it was merely the manner he adopted toward anyone with a title, even a baronet.

"Sir Jeremy," Mr. Hamm said effusively, holding out

a damp palm. Sir Jeremy shook his hand, with some reservations about its state of cleanliness.

"Well?" Sir Jeremy had no desire to prolong the interview.

"Do sit down, Sir Jeremy," Mr. Hamm requested. "What we have found out may prove very interesting to you."

Sir Jeremy raised an eyebrow as he seated himself rather awkwardly in the somewhat low chair. "Then you have discovered something new?"

"Oh, yes, yes, yes," Inspector Hamm said, smiling. He had a tight little mouth that appeared to be too small for even the passage of food. Doubtless, he lived on scandal, gossip, and crime, disdaining food as beneath his dignity. He seated himself behind his desk, the front of it concealing the fact that his feet did not quite touch the ground. "I hope you may soon be convinced that London has the finest police force in the world and that this department employs the finest men of that fine force."

Sir Jeremy grew impatient. "I never denied it," he said, untruthfully. "Come now, I don't have all day."

Mr. Hamm wrinkled his brow in a slight frown. He clicked his tongue. "Sir Jeremy, if you were a member of the noble force of the C. I. D. you would realize what an essential virtue patience is. An investigation of this nature requires a great deal of—" He hastily broke off as he saw Sir Jeremy's frown deepen. "Well, now, let's see what we have here." He took out a portfolio, thick with papers, a great many of them blank—just put in to thicken the case, as Inspector Hamm privately put it. He thumbed through them with great concentration, until he appeared to come across the exact one he was looking for, at which time his frown disappeared and his tiny mouth gave a tiny smile.

"Sir Jeremy," he said, barely getting the words out, since the smile was taking up so much of the limited space of his mouth, "I wish that I might be able to impress upon you the extreme beauty of this investigation. I might even call it brilliant. Martin—that's our man who's been working on the case—definitely has a bright career ahead of him, if this work is any indication."

"Yes, I'm sure he does," Sir Jeremy said. "Pray tell me of his brilliance."

"You know, of course, that we were unable to definitely prove who Miss X *is*, so Martin, with a stroke of genius, I must say, thought he might find out who Miss X *could be*." He paused to allow the brilliance of this idea to sink into Sir Jeremy's brain. "So simple, really," he continued, "but that's what makes it brilliant—just a matter of looking up some parish records."

"That's all very well," Sir Jeremy said, unimpressed, "but what does it mean?"

"It means, Sir Jeremy, that since we were unable to find out anything definite in France, we have turned our attention back to England." He leaned across his desk, ready to give a confidence. "We have discovered something very interesting about Robert Marsh, before he went to France."

"And that is?"

"And that is—he had a daughter of his own!" The inspector leaned back, eagerly watching for the effects of his disclosure.

"Ah," said Sir Jeremy.

"Indeed," said Mr. Hamm. "Do you see, Sir Jeremy? Our reports in France supported Miss X's story—we could discover no more than the fact that Robert Marsh had raised a daughter. However, we have now discovered that he had a daughter before he ever went to France." He consulted his notes. "According to this, she would have been about seven years old at the time of Robert Marsh's egress. That would make her—oh, about five and twenty now. Not impossible for her to pose as a seventeen-year-old. Sir Jeremy, do you see my point?"

"Yes, I see your point." All too clearly, he thought. So it was true, Alfie had been deceiving him all this time.

"Furthermore," Inspector Hamm went on, "according to the parish records, the name of Robert Marsh's daughter was Alfreda." He leaned forward again. "Now we don't use any names in a delicate case like this—that is, no more than necessary—but if the name means anything to you—well, there it is, eh?"

Sir Jeremy arose. "Yes, there it is. I must thank you for your work. I shall certainly speak with high praise of this department and Scotland Yard to anyone who will listen." He said this last with a slight sarcasm that was lost on Inspector Hamm, who took the words at face value and thought them well deserved. Sir Jeremy was suddenly eager to get away from the musty office and return to his club where he could think things out. He bowed slightly as he took his leave, and said, "I'm sure I needn't tell you that I wish this to be kept completely confidential."

Inspector Hamm was offended. "Sir Jeremy! You insult us. May I remind you that we are officers of the law, in the service of Her Majesty."

"Quite," Sir Jeremy said tersely. "Good day to you."

His thoughts were in a turmoil as he walked to his club, preferring not to take a hackney so that he might have more time to think. So, he thought, finally admitting to himself the full truth of his suspicions, Alfie is the daughter of the man who ran off with Caroline. And, obviously, she was quite as unscrupulous as her father, thinking nothing of posing as another man's daughter and ingratiating her way into his home and—dammit—into his affections. His initial anger lasted a few more minutes, but then his thoughts ran on to Alfie herself. Somehow the truth just didn't fit in with the Alfie he knew. From the first, when he had been hard put to believe her story, he had taken her character as evidence. And they had seemed to get on so well toegther; he had never known any other woman whose interests coincided so exactly with his own. Surely her very behavior couldn't be just part of the deception—no one could pretend so long or so well to share his interests just to further the ruse of relation. She had read all the books he recommended and expressed opinions of them that were close to his own; she had taken readily to his suggestions of learning to ride and to play chess; she had even acted as his hostess and welcomed his family with all the necessary affection he would expect from a daughter. He couldn't imagine Alfie as nothing more than a conniving female, out for his money.

But that's all she is out for, his other voice told him. Why else would she pretend to be eight years younger than she really is, deceiving not only him, but his entire family, and, if he allowed things to continue, all of England.

He did not doubt for a moment that Alfie was indeed Alfreda Marsh. It fit in too well—her apparent wisdom beyond her years, her poise, her unusual knowledge of the world, her very manner. And she couldn't possibly believe herself that she was born Alfreda Stafford; even if she had been only seven years old when her father took her to France, she must remember something of her early childhood in England, and certainly couldn't believe herself to be only seventeen. No, however much he wanted to believe otherwise, she had engineered the whole scheme and come to him with no other purpose than to fleece him of all he was worth.

"Damn!" Sir Jeremy exclaimed aloud, to the extreme disapproval of a few passersby. He wanted nothing so much as to drown his sorrows in some expensive brandy. "Damn my money," he said, this time to himself. It was the second time it had made him prey to a fortune-seeking female, and the second time the fortune-seeking female had the best of him. He wouldn't allow it, he would return to Stafford Hall and confront her with her guilt, he would make her extremely sorry she had tried to pull the wool over his eyes.

He almost smiled at the image that presented itself to him. He saw himself standing over her, pointing a long accusing finger, while she, sobbing, was on her knees, begging his forgiveness, begging for mercy. He would be exacting in his terms, he would made demands—perhaps force her to scrub the floors and clean the stables. She would be dressed in rags, and could see then how she fancied being the daughter of Sir Jeremy Stafford.

It was an impossible scene, he knew. How could he ever be unkind to her? No matter how much she had deceived him, he had become fond of her. No, it was worse than that—he had fallen in love with her. And with that admission his anger surged up again, and only his arrival at the door to his club prevented him from kicking a lamp post and undoubtedly inflicting more damage on his foot than on the recipient of his blow.

Unfortunately, Sir Jeremy was not destined to have that longed-for brandy immediately. Almost as soon as he set foot in the door a message was handed to him. He opened it with some annoyance, hoping it wasn't anything urgent, but soon discovered the contrary. There were only two lines, but the writing was bold and nearly half the words heavily underscored.

> Jeremy, come quickly. Something terrible has happened. Geoffrey is missing. I fear the worst.
>
> Cecily

Sir Jeremy's agitation was not as much as might have been expected from the tone of the message. He knew his sister's excesses of temperament well, and realized, wisely, that Geoffrey was most likely in no extreme danger. However, there was nothing he could do but go to the Chandlers' and find out what had happened. It wasn't so much the urgency of the summons as the lack of information it conveyed that prompted him to respond immediately—his curiosity was aroused and he saw a chance to take his mind off his other problems for the moment.

He found his sister distraught, as he had expected. In fact, she made an art of being distressed—she wore a flowing dark purple gown and a few strands of hair were in proper disarray. Her relief in seeing her brother was genuine, however.

"Jeremy! I'm so glad to see you!" she cried, running to him as he entered the morning room. "I have persuaded Richard to visit the police, although he seemed reluctant to do so. Imagine! Sometimes I think he has no more fatherly feelings than a turtle."

Sir Jeremy remained unruffled. "What is going on, Cecily? And I would like nothing so much as a brandy." Lady Chandler waved a hand at the dutiful Stuart, who poured Sir Jeremy his long-awaited drink, thoughtfully making it a large one.

Lady Chandler draped herself over a chair, the picture of motherly anguish. "I just don't know, Jeremy. He has simply *disappeared*. He left this note—here, I'll read it to you." She pulled out a small piece of paper, much blotted. " 'Important business. Will be back in a few days.' That's all he said, Jeremy. What do you suppose it could be?"

Sir Jeremy mulled over his brandy. "I suppose he had important business."

Lady Chandler gave an exasperated grunt. "You're as bad as Richard!" she said emphatically. "It was all I could do to get him to see the police, and even so he left only a few minutes ago. We may be too late already."

"Too late for what?" Sir Jeremy inquired. "Cecily, you speak as if he were running off to commit suicide."

Lady Chandler gave him a stricken look. "Perhaps worse."

"Cess, I have had a very trying day," Sir Jeremy said in a long-suffering tone. "Would you kindly tell me what is on your mind and stop behaving as if you were in a Restoration comedy."

She cast her eyes down. "This will be difficult for me to say, Jeremy, because it concerns you somewhat."

Sir Jeremy raised an eyebrow.

"It's my belief Geoffrey has eloped with Alfreda," she announced in tragic tones.

Sir Jeremy stood up. "What!" he said. "That's impossible!"

Lady Chandler changed from tragic to petulant. "Oh, I don't think so. Why, he's written her name all over his blotter. You should see it, it's a disgrace, all decorated with little hearts and arrows."

"Cecily, I am not interested in my nephew's infantile scribblings. A name written on a blotter does not signify that someone has eloped with the possessor of the name, even if that name is accompanied by the drawing of a heart."

"But, Jeremy, he went in the direction of Stafford Hall."

"My dear Cecily, I could name a dozen events of interest to Geoffrey that lie in that same direction. I'm afraid I'll need more substantial evidence before I believe this fairy tale."

"It was something he said to the groom as he left," Lady Chandler said. "Not something he *said* to him exactly, but something he was muttering in the groom's earshot." She paused, making certain she had her brother's attention. "He was muttering something about his cousin and getting married—nothing connected, you understand, but enough to make me believe—"

"I see," Sir Jeremy interrupted, sitting on the arm of a chair and ignoring his sister's resulting frown. "I suppose I must ride back to Stafford then, and see what has happened."

Lady Chandler brightened immediately. "Oh, thank you, Jeremy! I knew you'd see reason. You must stop them before it's too late."

"Cecily, there's nothing reasonable about construing a lot of unconnected remarks into an elopement, but I'll do my best." There was a note of bitterness in his voice. This news was another blow to his feelings toward Alfie. Evidently, he thought, she intends to firmly implant herself into this family—but still, the idea didn't fit her somehow. She had regarded Geoffrey as a silly little boy— Sir Jeremy had overheard her saying as much. Perhaps that was just another part of her game to throw off suspicion—although she must be a very sly player indeed, for she had seemed not to know that Sir Jeremy was listening at the time. He sighed. "If you are sending me after wild geese, Cess, I will be quite angry with you. I'm sure Geoffrey will turn up at some sporting place or other, but I'll chase after him just to humor you."

"I don't care what your motives are, Jeremy, just so long as you do it," Lady Chandler said firmly. "I don't like to say anything against your daughter, but it's just too bad of her. Geoffrey is so—so susceptible, if you know what I mean, and I don't think Alfreda has made it any easier for him."

"As far as I know, Cecily, Alfie did nothing but try to make it easier for him, as you say."

Just then Lord Chandler came in. "Well, I've reported it to the police, but I don't mind telling you, Cecily, that they nearly laughed me out of the place. Told me that if they were to concern themselves with every pair of fools running off together, they'd have no time left for important business. Oh, hullo, Jeremy." He held out his hand and shook Sir Jeremy's. "What do you think of this business?"

"I don't know," Sir Jeremy replied, "but I've told Cess that I'll go back down to Stafford Hall to find out whatever I can at that end. And if I find Alfie safe and sound there, someone will answer for it." This last remark was punctuated by a meaningful glance at his sister.

Lord Chandler laughed. "Right, just what I said. Still, it's no good letting him think he can run off without so much as a by-your-leave. Makes a boy cocky, I say. No, he can't be putting the household in an uproar whenever his fancy takes him."

"Quite right, Richard." Sir Jeremy smiled. "Although there's only one person in this household who seems to be in an uproar. However, I was planning to return to Stafford Hall shortly, since my business here is finished. Not quite so soon, though, since I just left there this morning."

Lady Chandler turned to him suddenly. "I didn't know that, Jeremy," she said. "You might have told me. I thought you had been in London all along. Tell me, did she seem peculiar, secretive in any way?"

"Of course not," Sir Jeremy said, and thought ruefully, no more than usual. "She didn't seem as if she were planning to leave very suddenly, although—" He remembered the quick kiss Alfie had bestowed on him the night before. Had she been trying to indicate something to him? It had seemed odd at the time, and now that he thought about it, it might have been a farewell kiss.

"Although what?" Lady Chandler asked.

"Nothing. Nothing at all. I'll leave as soon as I've had something to eat, Cess."

"I can't tell you what it means to me, Jeremy," she said with genuine gratitude.

"Well, why don't you show me by feeding me until I'm fat and stupid," Sir Jeremy suggested.

Lady Chandler laughed, feeling much better now that she had had her own way.

16

$\mathcal{A}$ LFIE lay back in the carriage seat, her eyes closed, occasionally fanning herself with a weak effort. She looked pale and deathly sick, but in fact she felt fine—or as fine as could be expected under the circumstances. Her faintness was a ruse to prevent Damon Whitfield from riding in the carriage with her. She couldn't bear the thought of being shut up with him for any length of time, and her threat that she was very prone to be sick in a closed carriage, especially if someone else was in it with her, had given her solitude. His vanity would not suffer the possibility that his puce and pink waistcoat might be sullied if he rode with Alfie, so, consoling himself with thoughts of the pleasures that would be his that night, he consented to ride beside the carriage and leave Alfie alone for the time being. However, he was constantly looking in the window at her, and thus it was necessary for her to appear ill, which she was doing very successfully.

Her hand could not resist stealing into her pocket occasionally, making certain that the item she had placed there was still safe. Alfie's anxiety that this item would be discovered too soon by Whitfield had made her forget momentarily any regret at leaving Stafford Hall, but now that she and it were safely on their way, she could think of little else but how happy she had been there and how much she would miss it.

She wondered how long it would be before Sir Jeremy became aware of her flight. She knew he was on his way to London at that very moment. It might take many hours, perhaps days, for the household to become aware that she was missing, for she had planned her escape carefully. Then it would be another few hours for a message to reach Sir Jeremy, and another few for him to return to Stafford Hall, if he did return at all. He might be reading her note later this evening, or early tomorrow morning, or sometime next week, depending on when he returned. By then she would be too far away for him to catch up with her and, she hoped, she would be rid of Whitfield as well and on her own once more. She reached into her pocket again. Yes, it was still there— in fact, it seemed to be the only solid thing on this very strange day.

Alfie had awakened early to the sound of Sir Jeremy's curricle taking him back to London and out of her life forever. She had arisen several minutes later, and the first thing she had done was write a note to Sir Jeremy. After several attempts, she remained unsatisfied with the result, but didn't have any time to improve upon it. She had an appointment with Damon Whitfield for which she could not be late.

He was precisely on time at their designated meeting place and Alfie could see him waiting impatiently in the distance as she rode to meet him. He was on foot, having left his carriage and horses on the road, out of sight from the house.

"Well?" he said as she came within earshot.

Alfie wasted no words either. "We shall leave today."

He bared a few tobacco-stained teeth in an attempt to smile. "Any time you are ready, my dear."

Alfie avoided his eyes. "Give me an hour to collect my things. You can pick me up at the south gate—it can't be seen from the house." She had no desire to prolong the interview, and so turned her horse immediately and rode back to the house.

Hawkins was in her room tidying up when she returned. She looked surprised to see Alfie back so soon.

"Why, miss, that was a short ride," she said.

Alfie smiled a bit nervously as she began to recite the lies she had so often rehearsed over the past week. Fortunately, Mrs. Jennings had unknowingly made this part of her tale a bit easier.

"Why, I met the Huxtables out riding and they've invited me to stay with them while Sir Jeremy is in London. Would you mind just packing a few things for me, I'll be leaving immediately."

Hawkins eyed her with a slightly suspicious glance, but did not reveal her surprise at the suddenness of this new arrangement. "Very good, miss," she said. "Shall I have the carriage brought round?"

"No, no, Hawkins. They were in a carriage and will

pick me up. Do hurry, please—I don't want to keep them waiting."

Hawkins signified her disapproval only by a muttering conversation she held with herself as she packed Alfie's things. The little bag was ready in a very short time as Hawkins was not permitted to put many things in it. By then, Alfie had changed from her riding habit to a traveling dress and a shawl—another thing that struck Hawkins as odd. However, she held her tongue, for it was not her place to say anything about the actions of her betters.

Alfie took the bag from her and gave her a sudden kiss on the cheek. "Thank you, Hawkins. You've been so good to me," she said and ran out the door and down the stairs. She paused only momentarily to leave her note on Sir Jeremy's desk and take something out of the desk, which she placed in her pocket. And now she felt in her pocket again for its reassuring presence.

The journey seemed interminable, and Alfie was beginning to feel ill in earnest by the time they stopped for a bite of lunch. She could hardly eat a mouthful, especially with the leering face of Damon Whitfield watching her across the table, noting her every move. She thought that she really would like to ruin his dreadfully bright waistcoat in the manner threatened, but since she had eaten nothing since the evening before, and then very little, that hardly seemed possible.

"I certainly hope you have recovered by the time we stop tonight," Whitfield said.

Alfie knew what was on his mind and shivered. "I sincerely think not," she replied in a low voice. "I feel as if I were ready to expire this minute."

"Well, we'll take care of that." He grinned. "I know of a way to make you feel better. My reputation as a master lover is not exaggerated, as you will soon discover for yourself."

Alfie wrinkled her nose. "I had not heard of that part of your reputation, only of your expertise in blackmailing and swindling, and your new occupation of kidnapping."

He gave a grunt of laughter. "I would hardly call it kidnapping, my love—rather a romantic elopement. But you will soon learn that I have other areas of expertise."

Alfie was growing very weary of his constant bragging— especially on this subject. She sincerely doubted that any lady had ever succumbed willingly to his advances. He had such a high opinion of himself, yet she was certain that the only way he could satisfy his lust was by either threatening a woman or paying her handsomely. Since Alfie's affections were not to be bought, with her he was using the former method. Alfie had thought she already hated him as much as she possibly could, but every minute she was forced to spend in his company had led her to discover another despicable thing about him. Again, her hand felt in her pocket and she almost smiled in spite of herself.

The afternoon was but a repetition of the morning's ride, long and intolerably boring. Alfie thought constantly of Sir Jeremy, wondering what he was doing at that moment, wondering whether he had learned of her absence yet, wondering what he would do about it. She sighed and tried not to think about him, for it only caused her more pain. She knew she would never see him again and it would be best if she could forget him as quickly as possible.

The evening found them in Dover, where Damon Whitfield immediately booked passage across the Channel for the next morning. They found rooms at a tolerable inn and Whitfield made sure of a private parlor for their supper. Alfie grew more and more nervous as the time when she would be left alone with him drew nearer, and her hand stole more and more often to her pocket.

Finally, that time came. The servants had brought in a large table full of food and had been ordered not to disturb them on any account. Damon Whitfield was almost rubbing his hands with glee and Alfie was disgusted at his eagerness. There was nothing she wanted less than to have him touch her—she would sooner die— and he acted as if a touch from him should cause a woman to swoon with ecstasy. She watched him with disgust as he stuffed food into his mouth, dribbling it onto the napkin that protected his prized waistcoat.

"And so, my little Alfreda, how are we feeling now?" Whitfield asked in his obnoxious tone of voice. He wiped his mouth on his hand and took a large drink of wine.

"I don't know how *we* are feeling, but *I* am not feeling very well at all," Alfie replied tartly.

"That's too bad, for it will make it all the more unpleasant for you, my dear," he mumbled through his food.

Alfie gave a disgusted snort. "As if anything could make it more unpleasant when it is already as unpleasant as it could possibly be."

"Aren't we bitter," he sneered at her. "Well, you'll soon change your tune. You may be unwilling now—in fact, I prefer you that way—but in a week or so you'll be begging for my attentions. Then perhaps I shall grow tired of you."

Alfie laughed at him. "As if I should ever desire your attentions. If I reached that point, I could do nothing better than to kill myself, for I should know that I had sunk to the lowest depths of humanity."

Damon Whitfield was not affected by this statement; instead, he seemed to relish it, for in his view it made the game more interesting. He helped himself to another serving. "We'll see what you say in a week or so, my dear. Especially after we've tied the proverbial knot."

Alfie looked at him narrowly. "So you are really going to marry me?"

"Of course, that was the point of this whole escapade— or one of the points." He sneered again. "Do you think I want to miss out on all of Sir Jeremy's lovely money and the position being the husband of the daughter of a respected country gentleman will give me?"

"What if I told you that I left Sir Jeremy a note, telling him who I really am?" Alfie asked tentatively.

"You wouldn't do that. You may feign all the innocence you like, but don't forget I knew your father and I know you for a scheming little minx, so I doubt you'd turn your nose up at whatever you can get." He waved his fork around to emphasize this point, before stabbing into a chunk of potato.

"What if I told you that I didn't care if I had the money, as long as you didn't have it?" Alfie said, a rising anger making her bolder.

"I would consider you to be a very stupid girl," Whitfield said. His plate clear again, he chose an apple from the pile of fruit before him.

"Do you really think you have anything to gain from this? Sir Jeremy is not such a fool as you think—he will never give you any money and he wouldn't introduce you to a scullery maid!"

This pronouncement had no apparent effect on Whit-

ield's calm demeanor. "Well, that would be too bad, but
erhaps more convenient in the long run because I would
ot be obliged to make you my wife and could retain my
urrent freedom." He crunched the apple between his
eeth.

Alfie watched him in a detached sort of way as he
consumed the fruit—core, pips and all. For a moment or
o, she forgot her personal danger and her former hatred
f the man, and saw before her only someone to be
itied. He was so sure of himself, so amazingly egotistical.
Ie really believed himself to be attractive and irresistible,
when in fact he was hardly more than a great lump of
issipated flesh. Suddenly Alfie was no longer afraid of
im, because for the first time she realized that he was
ot an inhuman monster, but only a rather fat, bad-tem-
ered, middle-aged man who had probably never known
appiness or joy and gave to the world only as good as
e had received.

"And what is going on behind those lovely eyes?"
Whitfield asked, his mouth dripping with juice from the
pple.

Alfie gave him one of his own sneers back. "I was
hinking what an object of pity you are. Sitting there
vith your smug self-satisfaction, displaying your boorish
able manners—you aren't even worth hating."

Whitfield finally grew angry at these remarks. He removed the napkin from under his chin and wiped his
mouth, leaving behind telltale traces of the dinner he
ad just consumed. "This has gone on long enough, my
lear. I shall wait no longer." He stood up.

Alfie stood up, too. "Yes, Mr. Whitfield, it has gone
n long enough." She reached into her pocket and pulled
ut the object of her previous attentions, pointing it

squarely at Damon Whitfield's heart. "If you take on
step toward me, I'll shoot you, Mr. Whitfield. It's a
simple as that." Her voice was amazingly firm considerin
how hard her heart was thumping.

Whitfield laughed loudly. "Aren't we fierce?" His voic
changed to a hiss. "You wouldn't dare to fire that, yo
haven't the nerve." He stepped toward her.

"Don't underestimate me, Mr. Whitfield," Alfie saic
and she pulled the trigger, not even certain where th
gun was pointed. He fell back with the shot, and Alfi
watched in horror as a puddle of blood formed on th
carpet where he had fallen. She dropped the gun and ra
over to him, to see whether she had killed him. No, h
wasn't dead, just shot in the arm. Alfie sat back on he
heels, relieved. As much as she loathed him, she woul
not like to think that she had actually killed someon
The big oaf had merely fainted from the pain and shoc
she thought, almost laughing. She heard some noises i
the hallway and acted quickly.

First she reached into his pocket and pulled out
pouch, heavy with gold coins. Strange, she thought, sh
had hated to steal as much as a dress from Sir Jerem
but she thought nothing of taking a bagful of gold fro
this person—in fact, she was happy to do it. Its weig
made her even happier as she realized she would n
soon starve with such a sum. She quickly concealed th
bag in her pocket just as the door opened and thre
members of the inn's staff entered.

Alfie stood up. "Send for the doctor quickly," sh
said. "The gun went off accidentally—I believe it's onl
his arm."

The inkeeper's wife immediately began muttering som
thing about "a respectable house" and "such goings on

but she managed to find time to send someone named Betty for the doctor.

"It's just his arm," the landlord said, bending over Whitfield. "Call Dick and we'll get him on a bed."

Dick was duly summoned and Alfie took the opportunity to slip away while they were preoccupied with transporting Whitfield's huge bulk into a bedroom. She didn't forget her small bag of clothes, and covering herself with a light shawl and tying her bonnet, she walked quickly out the front door, thinking with some satisfaction of what Whitfield's embarrassment would be when it came time to pay the shot.

Alfie made her way immediately down to the dock, which was not too distant from the inn, hoping desperately that the last packet had not yet left for France. She was in luck, she soon discovered; if she had been five minutes later, she might have been stranded until morning with the frightening possibility that Damon Whitfield would return to his senses and retrieve both his bag of gold and her. But her timing could not have been improved upon, for within half an hour of her pulling the trigger, she was on her way to France, with something much more comforting than Sir Jeremy's gun in her pocket.

She discovered suddenly that her appetite had returned and set about procuring a small amount of food and making herself comfortable on the deck, where the cool breezes of the sea eased her troubled spirits.

"How callous I am," she said to herself. "Less than an hour ago I nearly killed a man, and here I am taking the sea air and eating a dinner purchased with stolen money." But she felt no guilt for her actions—she would gladly shoot him again if the necessity arose. In fact, she felt somewhat like a champion of all the people Whitfield had ruined. No, *that* was something she need never regret; she already had too much to regret before she added shooting Whitfield to her list.

Thus her thoughts inevitably turned to Sir Jeremy. She tried to picture him in her mind's eye, what he was doing, where he was, to whom he was speaking. She thought of his funny crooked smile, wondered if he was smiling now, at this moment. She thought of the habit he had of raising one eyebrow and how many times she had longed to run her finger along the crease in his brow that formed when he did it.

She sighed and found she was unable to finish her small repast. She looked back toward the English shore, where a few flickering lights were still visible. She would never see it again, at least not for many years. Perhaps one day she might return when she was very old, to gaze once more on Stafford Hall as an outsider. There would be someone else living there then, a stranger most likely, or some distant relative of Sir Jeremy's to whom the estate had passed upon his death; someone who might have heard the tale of a woman who had once pretended to be Sir Jeremy Stafford's daughter. She might try to find out from some old tenant of the estate what had happened to Sir Jeremy and she might stroll once more through the well-loved fields.

Alfie felt a drop of wetness on her hand and realized she was crying. "Don't be silly," she reprimanded herself. "Three months ago you didn't know him and now you're out of his life and can act as if the whole episode never happened." Perhaps if she convinced herself that Sir Jeremy had merely been one of her dream heroes, she would feel better. One couldn't live one's life in love with a dream, could one?

Presently, Alfie made her way to her tiny cabin to rest for a while, uncertain of what the next day might hold.

17

SIR Jeremy arrived back at Stafford Hall after darkness had fallen. He was tired from having ridden hard, and he hoped fervently that his sister's suspicions were unfounded so that he might soon seek his bed. "And rest my weary head," he added to himself, thinking that the sort of rhyme Arthur Huxtable would appreciate.

Jamie was unable to hide his surprise at seeing his master back so soon, on horseback, and without any luggage nor even the groom who had accompanied him to London that morning.

"Well, Sir Jeremy," he said, taking the reins from him, "there do seem to be some queer goings-on today, make no mistake."

Sir Jeremy looked at him sharply. "Queer? Whatever do you mean?"

Jamie grinned. "Now, sir, if I knew they wouldn't be queer now, would they? But I suggest you ask Wilson about it. He'd know more than me, being in the thick of it, as you might say."

"In the thick of it?" Sir Jeremy repeated.

"Aye, sir. It's all a bit of a muddle and I can't explain it properly without confusing you more than you might be. Best consult Wilson, as I said."

"Thank you, Jamie, I shall do that," Sir Jeremy replied. "And you'd best get the black saddled and ready. If things are as you say, I may have a deal more riding to do tonight.

Jamie was amazed. "The black, sir? But—"

"You heard me correctly, Jamie. I hope it will not be necessary, but if what my sister thinks has indeed taken place, I'll need his speed." Sir Jeremy did not stay to hear any further protestations on Jamie's part, but strode toward the house, fearful that he would not see his bed that evening after all. Once in his study, he rang for Wilson, pacing around the room impatiently while he waited. Wilson arrived in a few minutes, and was much more adept at hiding his surprise at seeing Sir Jeremy and his condition of disarray than Jamie had been.

"You must excuse me, Sir Jeremy," he said. "I would have come immediately, but we did not expect you back quite so soon."

"Never mind that," Sir Jeremy said. "Where is Miss Alfreda?"

Wilson shifted his feet with an uncharacteristic fidgetiness. "She left early this morning, telling Hawkins she had been invited to the Huxtables, but—"

"But what?"

"Well, sir, this has been a most peculiar day." Wilson

cleared his throat, a bit of his distress showing through his reserve. "A short time after luncheon, Master Geoffrey arrived, asking where Miss Alfreda was. We told him she was spending a few days at the Jennings household and he left for there immediately. However, he returned a few hours later and said she wasn't there—in fact, the Huxtables weren't even there, having left for London. We sent for you immediately, sir, but as I said, did not expect you so soon."

"Damn," Sir Jeremy said in reply to this speech. A sudden thought occurred to him. "You say Geoffrey was looking for her?"

"Yes, sir," Wilson said. "He rode off again soon after he arrived. The second time, that is, sir."

"Where did he ride off *to*, in heaven's name?"

"Well, Sir Jeremy, it seems one of the stable boys saw Miss Alfreda enter a carriage at the south gate. I believe Master Geoffrey went in pursuit of that carriage."

"Stable boy?" Sir Jeremy's voice was rising in pitch as a result of his anxiety. "Send him to me, Wilson, and send in Hawkins as well." Wilson nodded and left immediately on his errand.

Left alone, Sir Jeremy resumed his pacing, at a slightly faster speed. So his sister was wrong, he thought. Geoffrey and Alfie obviously were not eloping together—not if Geoffrey was looking for her hours after she had already gone. But how had Geoffrey known she would be missing? He must have known something or he wouldn't have left London so precipitously to come to Stafford and inquire. Sir Jeremy realized he must have just missed his nephew on the road that morning, for Geoffrey had been leaving London just as Sir Jeremy was entering.

"Blast it," he said out loud, to no one in particular.

It was indeed a muddle, as Jamie had said. Just as he thought he had untangled all of Alfie's secrets, she had to go running off in this most uncourteous manner. He almost felt cheated of his just due—for by rights he should now be confronting her with her sins and demanding reparation. Where the devil had she gone? It was most inconsiderate of her. He had quite fancied himself as the noble injured party, doling out forgiveness like alms to the poor wretch who had wronged him. "Blast it!" he repeated, with more vigor than before.

Sir Jeremy hoped to gain some information from this stable boy so that he might follow Geoffrey in his mad pursuit. Finally tired of pacing, he sat down behind his desk. It was then that he noticed the small paper with his name written across it in neat, elegant handwriting. He picked it up eagerly and tore it open.

Dear Sir Jeremy,

As you read this I shall be far away from here. I have decided to return to France, and I hope that you will see the wisdom of my action.

It gives me great pain to write this note to you—almost as much pain as I have in leaving Stafford Hall, which I have come to love as my own home. Unfortunately, it is not my home and never can be, for I am no relation of yours, Sir Jeremy. When my father died—my real father, that is—I found the letter and locket which you now have in your possession. My original intention was to come to you as myself, giving you the locket and asking your aid in finding a teaching position for me in England. You see, I had no other friends in this country, but I always longed to return here, the scene of my happy childhood. I thought the information about your wife and child might be an introduction to your good graces.

However, somehow I thought of another plan. I am sure I needn't explain it—you have seen the results.

I realize now that my action was unforgivable. You

must believe me to be nothing more than a fortune
seeker, no better than I should be. I deserve such an
epithet, if not a worse one. Indeed, it would give me
great pain if you thought any better of me, because then
my actions could only have hurt you, too.

But it has become impossible for me to continue to
live a lie. Perhaps it would have been simpler had you
been an old man, as I expected, but feeling the way I
do about you, I can lie to you no longer. It is the coward
in me that forces me to disclose myself in this manner—
I could not bear to see your face as you read this, to
see you justly pointing an accusing finger at me. I have
removed myself from your life completely and I hope
that you will soon be able to forget me, although I will
never forget the happiness I knew at Stafford Hall.

> Yours faithfully (at last),
> Alfreda Marsh

Sir Jeremy read the letter quickly the first time and
then went back to read it a second time, more slowly. As
he read it the third time, a smile began to flicker across
his face, broadening as he came once more to the signature. It was a happy smile, quite unlike his ordinary
crooked smile of slight amusement. The crease that had
been on his brow since his meeting with Inspector Hamm
that morning disappeared and he felt as if the vise that
had been pressing his heart had suddenly been removed.
The insupportable vision of Alfie as out for all she could
get was firmly dispelled from his mind. A new vision replaced it—the picture of her looking at him in a troubled,
frightened manner, such as he had seen the day before.
She couldn't go through with it! She was not an unscrupulous fortune seeker as she called herself, but a lonely,
frightened girl, trying only to find some security for herself, and once she had found that security, she gave it
up again for fear of hurting him.

A quick knock disturbed his suddenly happy thoughts.

Wilson entered with Hawkins, looking red-eyed and miserable, and a young boy, looking frightened. Sir Jeremy laughed at the picture they presented.

"You needn't look as if you've just come before the Inquisition," he said. "Just tell me what you know and I'll be off. Wilson, do lay out a fresh shirt for me. I've been riding for hours in this one and soon you won't be able to tell me from my horse. Put a few things in a bag, too, I may be away for several days."

"Very good, sir," Wilson said, and he left.

Sir Jeremy turned to Hawkins. "Now what time did Miss Alfreda leave?"

Hawkins was feeling as if the whole thing were her fault for not questioning Miss Alfreda more carefully on her movements that morning. Since she had heard of Alfie's disappearance, she had been quite agitated and not a little tearful. She was twisting a handkerchief in her hands now as she replied to Sir Jeremy's question.

"Early, sir, and sudden like. It must have been close to ten o'clock."

"And what did she take with her?"

"Just a small bag, sir, filled with a few necessaries, if you know what I mean. Said she wasn't to be long and didn't want to take more than she deserved. Oh, Sir Jeremy," she wailed, "how was I to know?"

Sir Jeremy looked at her sharply. "Is that what she said, Hawkins? More than she deserved?"

"Her exact words, Sir Jeremy. I must say I thought it peculiar at the time, especially when she kissed me goodbye as if she were going on a long journey." With these words, she looked as if she was ready to burst into tears again. Sir Jeremy next spoke in a kinder tone with the hope of forestalling such an occurrence.

"If her actions struck you as peculiar, why didn't you do something about it?"

Hawkins' indignation at this remark got the better of her tears, and she replied, with some haughtiness, "Sir Jeremy, I'm not in the habit of telling my mistress what to do. I mentioned it to Cook, but she just said I was rattling on and mustn't disturb her with such nonsense."

Sir Jeremy sighed. "That's fine, Hawkins, you may go now." She started for the door, but Sir Jeremy noticed her stricken expression. "And thank you," he added. "I'm sure you couldn't have done anything even if Cook had paid attention. I certainly wouldn't blame you."

"Oh, sir," she said, the tears starting again in her eyes, "if I thought Miss Alfreda would come to any harm because I didn't speak up soon enough, I might as well end it all right now. She's a wonder, that girl, and you must bring her home safe and sound."

"I'll do my best," Sir Jeremy said gently.

Hawkins dropped a quick curtsy and left, blowing her nose into her handkerchief as she closed the door behind her.

During this time, some of the young boy's initial fears had left him, for he had been watching the scene as if it had all the fascination of a peepshow. But he was still certain he would fall down in a dead faint if Sir Jeremy so much as looked at him.

Fortunately, this did not happen as Sir Jeremy beckoned to him kindly. "Come here," he said. "There's a nice, shiny shilling for you if you tell me everything you saw." The boy hung back, tongue-tied. "What is your name?" Sir Jeremy asked him softly.

"Willie, sir," he said.

"Come over to me, Willie." Willie obeyed hesitantly,

fearing to do so, but fearing also to do otherwise. "Now I understand you saw Miss Alfreda leave in a big carriage. You can tell me, I won't hurt you."

The boy raised his eyes to Sir Jeremy. "Yes, sir," he said, "that's right, sir. Huge it was."

"Who was in the carriage?"

Having determined that he was not in immediate danger of being struck, Willie became a bit more at ease. "Why, this big man, sir. He was in the carriage. But then he got out when Miss Alfie said she'd vomit on him." He smiled suddenly at the remembrance of this exchange.

"Said she'd *what*?" Sir Jeremy asked, not certain he had heard correctly.

"Vomit, sir." The boy's smile widened. "She said riding in carriages made her sick, and riding with him would make her sicker. Oh, he didn't half like it, sir. All red he turned."

Sir Jeremy's brows creased. Was there yet another actor in this farce? "Were you able to hear where they might have been going?"

The boy did not hesitate now. "Yes, sir, as I told the other gentleman what asked, I think the big ugly man said something about they'd be safe and snug in France this time tomorrow. Then they took off down the Dover Road, sir, so I suppose that's where they were headed."

That made sense, Sir Jeremy thought. She had mentioned France in her letter, but the identity of the man was still a puzzle. He sighed, and reached in his pocket for the promised shilling to give Willie.

"Oh, thank you, sir!" Willie exclaimed, clutching the coin eagerly. "That's the second today!"

"Run along now. It's late and your mother is probably

worried about you," Sir Jeremy said, and Willie ran along.

Sir Jeremy stood up and stretched his tired legs, realizing that there was still a great deal of riding ahead of him. He put Alfie's letter in his pocket and went up to his room to change his shirt. Wilson had his things ready in a small bag that could be fastened to the saddle.

"Good luck, Sir Jeremy," he said. "We're all hoping you'll be bringing Miss Alfreda back to us soon. If you don't mind my saying so, sir, the changes she has brought about here have been nothing short of wonderful, and we'd miss her sorely."

"Thank you, Wilson, I'll need the luck. And I certainly agree with you." A very few minutes later Sir Jeremy was on his way, wondering what he would find when he came to the end of his journey.

It was a tedious ride, for while the black horse made good speed on the open stretches of highway, Sir Jeremy felt it necessary to stop at every inn along the way and inquire after Alfie or Geoffrey. He realized he was wasting a great deal of time when he met with no information, but he knew they must have changed horses along the way and thus there was a chance he would find something out, if only that he was following the right scent.

Toward midnight he came to a larger inn where he hoped he would have more luck, since it was a usual stopping point for travelers on the Dover Road. Indeed, he was correct; some of the members of the stable staff remembered changing horses for a huge carriage containing a fainting girl and accompanied by an ill-tempered gentleman on horseback. They had passed through a short time after one, and Sir Jeremy's heart sank as he realized he was nearly twelve hours behind them.

He went into the inn to bespeak some supper before he once again continued his search, and suddenly remembered that after hearing news of Alfie he had forgotten to inquire after Geoffrey. He saw the innkeeper standing nearby and went over to ask if he had seen his nephew.

Sir Jeremy described Geoffrey in great detail, but the innkeeper's face remained blank.

"Why, Father," an unexpected voice broke in, "that sounds like the gentleman in number five."

Sir Jeremy turned to see a very comely girl standing nearby. "He's staying here?" he asked eagerly.

The girl giggled. "I should think so—since he can't leave here." She noticed Sir Jeremy's puzzled look. "Why, he's broke his leg, sir."

This was not the most welcome news to Sir Jeremy. "May I see him?"

The landlord cleared his throat. "Well, if you were to be stating your name and business, perhaps—"

"I'm his uncle, dammit." Sir Jeremy grew annoyed. He was in no mood to be put off by the man, however well meaning his intentions toward Geoffrey.

The innkeeper's face cleared. "Oh, in that case, I don't see any reason why you shouldn't see him. Nan, go up and see if the gentleman's in a receiving mood, and show this other gentleman up to him."

Sir Jeremy murmured his thanks and followed Nan up to number five. It was indeed Geoffrey—a very sleepy Geoffrey—who looked at his uncle with amazement.

"I say, Uncle," he said. He made an effort to lift himself a bit, but was severely hampered by the splint on his leg.

Sir Jeremy turned to Nan, who seemed to be winking strangely at his nephew. "You may leave us."

"Yes, sir," she said, curtsying quickly and catching an answering wink from Geoffrey.

"What are you doing here?" Geoffrey asked, returning his attention to his uncle as the door shut.

"More to the point—what are *you* doing here, and with a broken leg?"

Geoffrey looked at him sheepishly. "I fell off my horse," he said. "Hurts like the devil."

"Most unfortunate." Sir Jeremy sat down on a nearby chair. "And now tell me how you knew Alfie would be leaving before she even left."

Geoffrey once again attempted to sit up a little straighter, but with a slight wince of pain gave up. "It was at the club last night. Damon Whitfield—"

"Whitfield!" Sir Jeremy exclaimed, jumping up from his seat. "So he's in this. I might have known! Go on, Geoffrey."

"Well, Whitfield was bragging about how he had an estate in the country now and soon he would have the daughter of a baronet to go with it. He didn't mention any names, of course—or I would have called him out then and there—but to anyone who knows you it was pretty clear who he meant."

There was an unpleasant set to Sir Jeremy's jaw that boded no good for Damon Whitfield. "Why didn't you send for me immediately?" he asked, tapping his foot with the general air of a stern schoolmaster.

Geoffrey was indignant. "Well, I did! I went right round to your club and found you'd gone back to Stafford Hall. I thought Alfie would be safe as long as you were there, so I went to bed, thinking Whitfield was just talking through his hat, as he has a habit of doing when in his cups. But this morning Mother was speaking as if she expected you for dinner so I realized you were coming back to London. I set out, hoping to find you at Stafford before you left, or at least pass you on the road, but as you know, I didn't. So I found out which way they went from some boy who'd seen the whole thing and—well, here I am."

Sir Jeremy's face softened, and he leaned against the wall, his arms crossed. "Well, Geoffrey, it seems you did your best."

"I jolly well did—and broke my leg for my troubles. Damn! You must go after them. If that beast—"

"Don't go on, Geoffrey. The thought is as unbearable to me as it is to you." He paused thoughtfully for a moment. "I just don't understand it—it seems as if she went willingly."

"Yes, that bothered me, too," Geoffrey said. "I thought she had more sense. But that Whitfield, perhaps he was threatening her—or you."

"That would be just like him," Sir Jeremy replied. He straightened himself with a resigned air. "I must leave immediately."

"Do—I might have caught up with them, but I'm afraid it's almost too late now."

"So am I. By the way, have you sent word to your mother about what has happened to you?"

"Oh no!" Geoffrey exclaimed, striking his brow with his hand and presenting quite a comic consternation. "I completely forgot, what with all the excitement."

"Yes, the excitement showed me up here, as I recall," Sir Jeremy said with a faint smile. "I suggest you do so immediately. She is under the impression that you have eloped with Alfie."

Geoffrey leaned his head back and laughed. "I say,

that's good! I suppose I must put her mind at ease. Doesn't she know by now that Alfie wouldn't have me?"

"I'm just glad that you've finally realized it," Sir Jeremy said sternly, unable to share Geoffrey's amusement. "I'll go now. By the way, have you enough money?"

"Yes, I stuffed my pockets before I left, not knowing how far I'd have to go," Geoffrey said. "Good luck."

"Thank you, I'm afraid I'll need it. And I suggest that you rest well, you look like the very devil. And Geoffrey," he continued, once again in his role as schoolmaster, "don't be giving your mother worse cause for worry, if you know what I mean."

Geoffrey grinned. "I know I'm green, sir, but not so green as that. But isn't she nice, though? And she's been ever so attentive."

"A regular little angel at the gates of heaven, eh?" Sir Jeremy said, and left before Geoffrey could make further comment.

18

SIR Jeremy continued his interminable journey with
a fresh horse procured from the inn's stable. It was not
a mount he would have chosen for himself, for it had a
somewhat heavy and plodding gait; nevertheless, it was
fresher than Sir Jeremy himself, and while it didn't have
the speed of the black, he actually made better time on it
than he had during the first half of the night since he was
no longer making frequent stops at inns along the way
to inquire after Alfie—not only because it was his intention to reach Dover as soon as possible, but also because
the hour was very late and it was a rare hostelry that still
had some lights twinkling at the windows.

As he rode, he pondered the question of why Alfie had
gone willingly with Damon Whitfield. Sir Jeremy's attitude toward his erstwhile daughter had changed many

times in that day, but he could not reconcile this newly discovered action of hers with any of his conceptions of her—especially the one he hoped was true. In fact, he could imagine no woman finding anything desirable in Whitfield, except perhaps his money. Sir Jeremy shuddered at the thought of what a woman would have to do in return for that money—surely Alfie couldn't be hardened enough to sell herself so.

He smiled suddenly, remembering Willie's description of Alfie's departure—to ride with Whitfield would make her sick, she had said. That sounded like the Alfie he wanted to believe in. And yet, the fact remained that she *had* gone with Whitfield. The only possible solution was the one Geoffrey had suggested—Whitfield must have used some sort of threat to force Alfie to agree to this flight.

Sir Jeremy was very weary and these thoughts only succeeded in giving him a headache. "Damn," he said to himself, not for the first time. "Why am I even going after her? Why don't I just leave her to her fate, let her go where and with whom she pleases?" Unfortunately, he knew too well the answer to these questions—he could not live without her. Even in the moments of his worst thoughts about her, she had still been present to receive his wrath, if anything. In his mind, he had denounced her, railed at her, even struck her, but he had never sent her away. And in the moments of his best thoughts about her, he had seen a snatch of what he had always wanted— an intelligent, beautiful wife, with a wit that would never bore and a warmth that would never wane. He knew that Alfie could provide all he had ever sought in a woman, and he needed her, needed her desperately.

There was no alternative, he must find her. He would

take her back under any conditions, even if—once again Sir Jeremy shuddered—yes, even if Whitfield had already taken advantage of her. Alfie had become too much a part of his world, and he would do anything, forgive anything, to have her safely back in that world. Never once did Sir Jeremy think that she might not wish to return with him; instead he thought of the look in her eyes when he sometimes caught her gazing at him, the quick kiss she had given him the night before, the phrase in her letter, "feeling the way I do about you." Of course she would come back with him. He kicked his horse, eager to reach Dover.

It was nearly dawn by the time Sir Jeremy arrived in that city. By then only one thought remained uppermost in his mind—that Alfie had been unable to resist Whitfield's advances. He could not imagine her submitting willingly, even though he knew she had entered the coach willingly—but not until she had made certain she needn't share it with Whitfield. Willing she had been, not stupid. But what had happened when the coach had reached its destination and she could no longer take refuge in it? Whitfield would stop at nothing to get his way, Sir Jeremy well knew, and he thought of a hundred things that might have happened to Alfie, each one worse than the last.

Sir Jeremy once again started to make inquiries at inns, dispensing coins to anyone who tried to help him. If they had not spent the night in Dover, this would once again be wasted time, but he could not run the risk of missing them altogether. He began with the largest, most fashionable hotel and worked his way down from there.

He was in luck this morning. At the third place, in answer to his questions, he was treated with a long story of someone shooting somebody and somebody furious when he awoke because someone had shot him and run off with all his money, and he certainly weren't no light-weight when they had to carry him to the bed and he was only shot in the arm for all that. The humor of the tale alone would have been worth Sir Jeremy's time and coins, but as he asked for details, it seemed more and more certain that his quest was ended.

"And you say this woman has disappeared without a trace?" Sir Jeremy asked the boy whose powers of story-telling were almost without parallel.

"Oh, yes, sir, gone she was like a ghost in the night. Some folks think she *was* a ghost, or a witch at the very least, she disappeared so sudden."

Sir Jeremy's pleasure had increased with every embell-ishment of the tale, but he was not too happy with this last information. Gone again? Where to this time?

"Do you know this man's name?" he asked with a sigh.

The boy's eyebrows raised in interest. "Are you from the C.I.D.?" he asked eagerly.

Sir Jeremy smiled. "Not really. Let's say I'm an in-terested party, if this is indeed the man I am seeking."

The boy wiped his nose, disappointed. He would have welcomed a police investigator to relieve the boredom. "Ask *her*," he said, indicating the person referred to with a jerk of his thumb.

"Thank you," Sir Jeremy said, ready to give the boy a coin for his troubles, but he had already gone off to regale another interested party with his tale. Sir Jeremy walked over to the woman indicated, seemingly the landlady.

"Madam," he said graciously, "I understand you have an injured man here. May I inquire as to his identity?"

The woman looked at him suspiciously. "And what's he to you?"

"I understand he has been relieved of his money. I thought I might assist—"

Her suspicion vanished immediately. "You should have said so! That's Mr. Whitfield up there—shot in the arm only, but can't move a muscle to help himself, as if he were shot straight through the heart. And it might have been better so, the Lord forgive me for saying. It was an unlucky day when that man came under my roof." She sniffed. "Imagine the fairy tale he's telling, as if that young lady what come with him had overpowered him single-handed and robbed him of his money, so now he can't pay me for my troubles. A great huge man as that telling such a story, just because he can't pay the reckoning. It's no good for the reputation of my establishment, I must say, and I'd turn him out in a minute if he weren't injured and I weren't a Christian woman." As she spoke, she led Sir Jeremy up the stairs to the door of Whitfield's room. "Just you wait here and I'll announce you like, though the likes of him don't deserve such courtesies, for all his high-born airs."

A few moments later Sir Jeremy was treated to the sight of Damon Whitfield laid out in a bed that looked as if it would fall apart any minute under his weight. His arm was wrapped in bandages from the wrist to the shoulder, and the look on his face was not pleasant. Sir Jeremy could not help laughing at the sight.

"What is it, Stafford?" Whitfield growled. "Stop that racket and state your business."

Sir Jeremy tamed his laughter to no more than a small grin. "So you were going to make me sorry, Whitfield?"

"And I will, too, damn you—I'll have her prosecuted

and hanged for attempted murder and robbery."

Sir Jeremy chuckled again. "It would never stand in a court of law. One look at you and one look at her and they'd laugh you into the street for your troubles. Even your landlady doesn't believe the charge, and from what I understand, she was one of the first to find you in your present—prostrate—state. I was treated with a very delightful version of the tale just now."

Whitfield only grunted.

"No," Sir Jeremy continued, "I think a charge of forcible abduction would carry much more weight."

"You wouldn't dare," Whitfield snarled.

"It's not that I wouldn't dare, but that I wouldn't want Alfie's name connected in any way with yours."

Whitfield gave another grunt, this time of laughter. "Alfie's name," he repeated in a mincing tone. "And what name is that, my dear Sir Jeremy?"

"That of Alfreda Stafford," Sir Jeremy replied, seeing perfectly well what Whitfield was up to.

"Alfreda Stafford, indeed," Whitfield said, and he played what he thought was his trump card. "She's no more your daughter than I am." He leaned back, a triumphant glare on his face.

Sir Jeremy feigned surprise. "Why, whoever said she was my daughter?" he said. "I mean Alfreda Stafford, my wife."

Whitfield's face showed sufficient astonishment to satisfy Sir Jeremy. "Your wife! What kind of trick is this, Stafford?"

"Trick?" Sir Jeremy was the picture of guileless innocence. "Why, no trick at all. In fact, I believe it's what you once referred to as marital joy."

"Get out of here, Stafford. Get out of here now!" Whitfield made an attempt to raise himself, but failed, the bed creaking precariously as he fell back onto it.

Sir Jeremy stood up in a leisurely fashion, enjoying every moment. "I leave with pleasure," he said. "But now it's my turn for a warning, Whitfield. If Alfie's name is even mentioned by you again, I will come and personally shoot you in the other arm—or perhaps a more vital area. And don't think I won't hear of it, either. I don't have to pay for the loyalty of my friends." With that he left, feeling very satisfied indeed with the interview.

He realized he wanted nothing so much as something to eat, so feeling more lighthearted than he had in years, Sir Jeremy went down to the dining room and ordered a hearty breakfast. As he ate, the results of nearly twenty-four hours of riding and sleeplessness made themselves known to him in an obvious manner, as every aching bone in his body seemed to cry out for rest. His journey was not yet ended, but he could not continue until he had had some sleep. Alfie was no longer in any personal danger, so he felt he could afford to postpone further searching until he had recovered somewhat from his arduous journey from London to Stafford to Dover.

With that in mind, he obtained a bedroom, ignoring the objections of the landlady that gentlemen requiring rooms in broad daylight ruined the reputation of her establishment. He was asleep almost before his head touched the pillow, waiting only long enough to read Alfie's letter again.

He awoke some six hours later, feeling quite refreshed. It was just one o'clock when he descended to the dining room for a light luncheon. Whitfield, he learned, was still laid up, but—to the landlady's delight—had sent to London for funds. She was even more delighted when Sir

Jeremy paid his bill readily, with a bit extra thrown in so the reputation of her establishment wouldn't suffer overly much, and he was soon on his way to continue his pursuit of Alfie.

Alfie sat on a stone bench in a shaded park, a few stray autumn breezes ruffling her hair. She was reading a French novel she had purchased in a book shop the day before, but was finding it difficult to keep her mind on the words, preferring to watch the actions of some squabbling birds and chittering squirrels. Her thoughts constantly wandered to Sir Jeremy, and more than once she attempted to wrench them away and concentrate on the book in her lap. But that was a romance, and the hero was so unkind as to bear a striking resemblance to Sir Jeremy; oddly enough, it seemed all the male characters in the book looked like Sir Jeremy, and the book could not help but defeat its own purpose in taking Alfie's mind *off* Sir Jeremy.

She had been in France nearly a week now, traveling around, stopping at various schools to see if they desired or required her services. She had had no luck as yet, but was not immediately concerned, for the sum of money she had found in Whitfield's purse was enough to keep her for a year if she lived frugally. However, she hoped to find some occupation soon, if only to take her mind off the events of the past several months.

She smiled as she thought of the charm her strange past held for some of the French schoolmistresses she had been interviewed by. They looked sharply at her expensive clothes, and even more sharply into her face when she said that she had no references, no family, no home. Here indeed was a mystery. One headmistress seemed almost ready to hire her on the strength of the mystery alone, feeling certain that Alfie would have some interesting secrets to reveal when the time came, but she had thought better of it as she explained that they were already overstaffed.

Alfie had decided to remain a few days in this particular town because it was such a peaceful and pretty place and boasted mineral water that would cure anything from a broken bone to a broken heart. Alfie tried to convince herself that it did not remind her of Stafford, mineral water excepted, but was unsuccessful. In fact, everything seemed to remind her of Stafford, just as every time she saw a man who walked like Sir Jeremy, or had the same shoulders, or cut his hair in the same style, her heart would jump to her throat until the man turned around and proved himself not to be Sir Jeremy. In fact, this was happening at that very moment as she noticed a man with Sir Jeremy's forceful stride walking through the park.

"Silly," she told herself, "how long will it be before this stops happening?" But the feeling of recognition persisted as she watched this man walking back and forth, apparently searching for someone. Eventually, he looked in her direction, and oddly enough, stared toward her.

Alfreda stood up as he came closer, her book dropping unnoticed to the ground. She felt the thumping of her heart grow faster as he approached, for he had not yet proven himself not to be—

"Alfie!" he called.

"Sir Jeremy?" she whispered. She could not move, she could only stand there and watch him come toward her. Finally, when he was only a few feet away, she ran the last few steps toward him as if drawn by a magnetic force. Instantly, they were in each other's arms, Alfie resting her head against his shoulder as she had so often longed to do.

A few moments later, though, she broke the spell, backing away from him. "How did you find me?" she asked.

Sir Jeremy smiled down into her wondering gaze. "It wasn't easy," he said gently, "but I was very persistent."

Alfie stared at him, dazed, hardly daring to believe that he was really there. "But how could you—why did you—?" She dropped her eyes. "I thought you would hate me for what I did."

Sir Jeremy took her hands in his. "I could never hate you, Alfie. I was angry with you for lying to me, and then I was disgusted with you when I thought you had gone willingly with Whitfield, but I never hated you." He placed a finger under her chin and raised her face to his once more. "On the contrary, even when I thought the worst of you, I knew I couldn't live without you."

Alfie felt like laughing and crying all at once. She could say nothing and merely continued to gaze at him, a look of supreme joy on her face.

Sir Jeremy returned her look gravely. "I realize, of course, the risks involved by taking you back with me. You have left quite a trail of casualties behind you."

Alfie raised her chin proudly. "I was glad to shoot him. It was one of the noblest things I've ever done, and I'd do it again tomorrow."

"I agree completely, but poor Geoffrey."

"Geoffrey? What has he to do with this?"

"There, you see? You have no idea what destruction you have wrought. I feel as if I've joined some charitable club designed to visit the sick and injured." Sir Jeremy's tone was light, but Alfie was puzzled by his words. He continued. "My nephew saw himself as the knight in shining armor, and took it upon himself to try to save his lady fair—that's you—from the dragon. Unfortunately, the stalwart knight fell off his less-than-trusty steed and received a broken leg for his troubles. He is now recuperating in a wayside castle, a fair peasant maiden tending to his every want and whim."

"Oh dear!" Alfie was not sure whether to laugh or be distressed by this news. "Poor Geoffrey. But how did he find out I was leaving?"

"Our noble knight heard the dragon bragging the night before, and being an astute young mathematician, with the aid of his fingers he put two and two together."

Alfie could not help but abandon all tender feelings and laugh at Geoffrey's plight. "It's terrible—I feel so terrible for him. Do let me go back and shoot Whitfield again, this time for Geoffrey."

"Don't worry, I've already threatened him with that fate." Sir Jeremy grew serious once more. "May I ask you something, Alfie?"

She nodded.

"What did you mean by 'feeling as you did about me'?"

"I meant, well, I meant—" She searched his face again and decided she might as well speak the truth. "I meant that I had fallen in love with you."

With a strong gesture Sir Jeremy crushed her in his embrace. "I hoped that's what you would say! Oh, my darling, I love you, too, and I will not rest until you are my wife."

"Your wife?" Alfie murmured, still not quite believing this was happening to her.

"Why, of course. It wouldn't do for you to return with

me to Stafford as my daughter. There would be talk when the babies came."

"But what can we tell them? How can we explain?" Alfie's voice was muffled by Sir Jeremy's shoulder.

"Ah, I've thought about that, you know," Sir Jeremy said. "We'll tell them that you truly believed you were my daughter, and when you discovered you were not, you became so distressed that you immediately returned to France. And being an honorable man, I, of course, had to follow you and marry you so you would not be burdened for the rest of your life with the shame of having lived under the same roof with a man you were not married to."

Alfie bent her head back to look up at him. "Dear, dear Jeremy, do you forgive me for what I did? It was despicable, I know—but can you forgive me?"

In answer, Sir Jeremy gave her a long and forceful kiss, thinking to himself that if this didn't convince her, he would be glad to give further proof.